MW01074312

Found in Embers

Astrid Stone / Book One

The Writing Ranch LLC.

Cover Design by Covers by Combs

Editing by Janeen Ippolito

Proofreading by Charis Emrich

Print ISBN 978-1-959977-01-8

Ebook ISBN 978-1-959977-00-1

For Mom.
For reading and treasuring
everything I've ever written.
And for giving me great genes.
(After all that, you deserve it!)

FOUND
IN
EMBERS

ASTRID STONE BOOK 1

AJ BLANCH

THE WRITING RANCH LLC

ONE

"Order up!" The call bell rang, but I ignored it. My head was fuzzy with another migraine coming on despite having taken my medication this morning. I silently cursed the rainy spring weather which always made the episodes more frequent.

"Order up!" The cook hit the bell twice.

"Okay, I'm coming!" I eased my body up from the box I'd been using as a seat in the corner of the kitchen. I glanced at the clock—just two hours until my shift was over. I mentally calculated the cost of taking an extra dose of meds and how long it would be before I could afford to spend grocery money on more.

Just push through it, Astrid.

Grabbing my serving tray, I loaded it up with the food that was waiting in the window, along with a handful of napkins that boasted the slogan "best bbq in KC!" The words blurred, and I grabbed the stainless steel counter to steady myself against the sudden dizziness.

Ugh, please. Not now, not here.

Two deep breaths. I shook my head to clear it. The episode was subsiding, but I didn't trust myself to move yet, so I played for time by grabbing a squeeze bottle and drizzling sauce artfully onto the food that had been unceremoniously slopped into the serving boats. Art always calmed me—it was both my passion and my coping mechanism.

"It ain't a gourmet," growled the cook in my direction from the other side of the window. "Just get it to the customer." I often wondered if the hair net covering his meticulously trimmed beard was what made him so grumpy at work.

"Presentation is important." I smiled, though I knew it would irritate him more.

"It's burnt ends," he said, slapping his spoon on the counter. "You can play with your food at home."

Jen, a fellow server, waddled in through the dining room door and dumped a bin of dishes in the sink. "Astrid honey, can you take the order for table 5? They asked for you specifically."

"What? No they didn't." I looked between Jen and the swinging metal door in confusion.

Jen put one fist on her large hip. "They asked for, and I quote: 'That pretty server with dark hair that was here yesterday.'" She looked at me pointedly. "Besides, I gotta get a smoke break 'fore the boss come up in here."

She winked and headed towards the back door.

My pounding head searched my memory banks for who had been here yesterday. *Hopefully it's not the couple that didn't leave a tip.*

I picked up my tray and called after her. "If it was anyone but you, Jen..."

"You know you love me!" She waved without looking back.

She was right. She made this job far less miserable.

Two men in military uniform sat on either side of table 5, their heads bent in conversation. One was much older, with salt and pepper hair. The younger soldier was extremely well built and sun kissed—with his sandy hair and sharp jawline—he had a cowboy look about him. They definitely hadn't sat in my section the day before. I would have remembered serving a hot soldier.

After delivering the burnt ends to the woman at table 12, I pulled the order pad out of my apron and started towards table 5. The cowboy soldier looked up, and his face lit with a smile as I approached. His eyes tracked my movements across the room. I glanced around, uncomfortable with the attention.

I wish I had let Jen take care of her own table. Admiring from across the room, and having to interact with this man were two very different things.

I arrived at the table avoiding eye contact with Cowboy, my eyes landing on his name tag which read MILLER.

They knew what they wanted, so the order didn't take long, but my migraine episode seemed to be getting worse again. Blind spots in my vision made it tricky to write the words down, and the cacophony in the room started to sound like it was in a tunnel. I blinked a few times, trying to see the pad more clearly. When dizziness overwhelmed me, I put a hand on the back of the closest bench, trying to be casual about it. The blond soldier continued to smile at me from what I could tell. Since my mind was trying to fill in the gaps of my vision, I couldn't exactly be sure.

"Astrid?" When Miller said my name, I realized he had been speaking to me. "Are you okay?" Terror clenched in my gut.

How do these strangers know my name?

Then I remembered that I was wearing a name tag and told myself not to panic. I glanced down to reassure myself. I could only see the A that was etched in the plastic because of the spots in my vision. But knowing it was there calmed my frantic heart.

"Are you okay?" Miller asked again.

"Yeah." It came out breathy. The cold sweat started, a symptom that often came with these episodes. I swiped the back of my hand across my clammy forehead, practically poking my eye with the pen in my hand.

"Um," I cleared my throat, realizing that I was acting super awkward. "Yeah I just—wondered if I could get you anything else?"

He chuckled a bit. I worried my lingering at their table seemed like I was trying to flirt, but I couldn't walk away until I felt steadier.

"You, uh, drew on your face a bit with that pen." The cowboy gestured to his face, which I could hardly see from the blind spot. Embarrassment crashed over me in a wave. I let go of the bench to scrub at my face with my other arm. Bad idea—without the anchor, I felt myself sway. Miller grabbed my pen-wielding arm as he stood, suddenly towering far too close to me. His masculine scent of earthy leather and citrus overwhelmed me. All I could see was his broad chest inches from my face. My heart started racing. There I was, at twenty-three and I'd never been this close to a man before, let alone an attractive one. The feeling in my stomach was strange. I couldn't tell if it was from the episode or from having a man so close to me. He had both hands now wrapped around my biceps. Afraid of the sudden intimacy of the contact, I flinched and he let me go, his hands up in a surrender gesture.

"I'm sorry," he said. I would have found the slight drawl in his voice charming if I hadn't been distracted by an overwhelming need for self-preservation. "It just seemed like you were about to fall."

The room spun, and I grabbed his arms before I bit the floor.

"Maybe you need to sit." The older soldier gestured to a nearby chair.

Sitting or not, I knew from experience what was coming and I stumbled back, mentally kicking myself for not just taking the extra medicine.

Oh my god, I cannot pass out in front of all these people. It was my only clear thought as I bumbled towards the bathroom, using the chairs along the way for support.

The single little unisex bathroom in the back corner of the restaurant was occupied. I cursed. A tremor of nausea accompanied the dizziness. Only a few steps to get to the kitchen, I clutched the wall like it was a lifeline. Beyond the kitchen door hung my bag that contained my medicine. The blind spots still obscured my vision, but I noticed grease residue on the swinging door as someone opened it into my face. Then everything went black.

I came back to hazy consciousness with Jen's voluminous form hovering over me.

I was sprawled on the dining room floor, having not quite made it to the kitchen.

"Astrid, where your meds at?" Jen asked.

"My bag." I reached up to touch my cheek where it throbbed.

Jen worked to get off the floor. "I'll get 'em for you."

"Are you okay?" It was the cowboy's drawl. I turned to focus on the soldier, his cerulean eyes narrowed in concern. With my blind spots mostly gone now, I could read his expression clearly.

I started to sit up, but he put his hand on my shoulder— a subtle command. "Careful, you hit your head."

It was embarrassing enough having anyone see me pass out. I didn't need someone to keep me here on the floor.

"I'm fine." I sat up against his wishes.

"Can you tell me your name?"

"Astrid." I shivered involuntarily. I looked down to find goosebumps on my arms, and noticed I was covered in baked beans and burnt ends.

My face flushed with embarrassment.

"How many fingers am I holding up?" Miller's fingers were long, and his nails were clean and trimmed.

"Three," I answered him.

"How about your phone number?"

I scowled at him. "I'm not telling you my phone number."

He smiled shamelessly and winked at me. "It was worth a shot."

"Girl, you can't keep comin' to work like this," Jen said as she returned with my tattered bag and held out the bottle of medicine,

"You probably need to see a doctor after hitting your head like that," Miller added.

I ignored him and turned towards Jen. "It's just the rainy weather." I took the bottle. "Rain makes the migraines worse. I'll be fine."

"I'm glad to hear that you're okay, Miss Stone." The booming voice of Mr. Strickner sent another chill through me. "I'd like you to collect your things and go home."

I scrambled up to face my perpetually grouchy boss. My head spun from the movement. "I'm fine. I can finish my shift."

"You're a liability in my kitchen. I want you to go home."

"I'm sorry, Mr. Strickner. It was a freak accident. It won't happen again."

"No, it won't." His voice was cold and quiet. "You can pick up your final check on Friday."

"Wait, you can't fire me." I leaned in, aware of the people watching. My face burned with shame when I added, "Please, I need this job to make rent."

"I'm sorry for your difficulty, but it's not fair to any of my other employees to have to pick up the slack every time you get a migraine."

Next week was Lyric's Sweet 16. Money was already

tight. Desperation rose in my chest. "Please, I have my little sister to feed."

He turned and walked away, ending the conversation.

Ugh, he's such a jerk.

Anger and shame burned through me as I stood there, covered in barbecue, with everyone watching.

I rubbed my thumb over the amber stone in my leather cuff, a nervous habit I'd carried with me from childhood—it helped to calm me.

My eyes stung with the injustice of it all.

I started towards the front door, wanting to get outside before there were tears—or worse.

Jen caught my arm and gave it a little squeeze. "Baby girl, you got too much talent to waste at this place anyway." She held out my bag to me.

"Thanks," I said, taking it. "It would've been embarrassing to have to come back in for my car keys."

She snorted, and put her fists on her hips. "You best toughen up that skin of yours if that was gonna get to you."

I gave her a half smile. "I'll miss you."

"I ain't dead, and you've got my number."

"You're right. I guess I'll see you sometime."

I glanced at the soldier who was still standing there, worry written in his features. He looked like he was going to say something, but I shook my head.

"Please, don't make it worse."

I pulled my serving apron off and handed it to Jen. "Their order is on my order pad," I said, nodding towards table 5.

. . .

When I stepped outside, the air smelled of wet pavement and the hickory smoke rising from the stack.

Wrapping my arms around my bag to protect it a bit, I stepped into the rain and jogged to my rusted-out handicap van.

Seeing my face in the reflection of the water-streaked window, a chunk of sauce-covered pork sliding down my cheek, felt like a new low.

What is wrong with me?

The despair and anger burned my eyes, or maybe it was the barbecue sauce.

Tears began to spill over my cheeks, mixing with the rain.

I swiped at the slop on my face, bringing the hem of my shirt up to scrub at my eyes.

"Hey." It was he cowboy soldier's voice.

I whipped around, yanking my shirt down.

Why is he following me?

"Sorry, I didn't mean to startle you," he faltered.

"What are you doing here?" I glanced around.

Can't a girl lose her shit in private?

"I wanted to give you your tip." He offered me a folded-up bill.

I waved it away. "You can tip Jen. She's your server."

"Don't worry. I'll tip her too." He kept his offer extended even as the rain soaked us both.

"I don't want your pity." I cursed my pride. Every dollar mattered until I could find another job.

He rubbed the back of his neck with his free hand. "It's not pity, I promise. Just take it."

Swallow your pride, Astrid. Take it for Lyric.

Drawing in a shaky breath, I took it and mumbled a

thank you. As I turned to open my door, the soldier spoke again.

"I... actually didn't come here for the food." I looked at him warily. "I have pepper spray."

His hands came up in surrender, and he rocked back on his heels a bit. "I'm not trying to seem like a creep."

"Well here's a tip: it's creepy to follow a girl to her car in the rain."

"Yes Ma'am." He nodded. "My superior officer did advise against it."

I raised an eyebrow at him. "Coming here when you don't even like barbecue—also creepy."

He winced. "No, I mean I love barbecue, but we had it yesterday—I still have the leftovers in my fridge."

I held up the pepper spray attached to my keychain. "Are you stalking me?"

"No! No, I just noticed you here yesterday and wanted to introduce myself, but my buddy needed help, so we left before I got a chance."

It felt kind of surreal that he had come here specifically to meet me. I felt a little guilty. The guy clearly had no idea that I was not emotionally available and wouldn't be for the foreseeable future.

He seemed nice. Still, the over cautious part of me kept the pepper spray between us.

"Please don't spray that." He gestured to my weapon of choice. "With the wind and the rain, you're more likely to hurt yourself than me."

He was right. I lowered the spray.

"Hey, I'm sorry about your job." He hitched a thumb at the restaurant behind him. "The boss seemed real nice too."

I laughed once without humor. "Yeah."

"Things have a way of working out."

I smiled. "My mom used to say that."

"Well, she's right."

She's gone. It was hard to remember the sound of her voice. But the reminder of her words lifted my spirits. I rubbed my thumb over the stone in the cuff—her cuff.

"Thank you." I said. Meaning it this time.

Gesturing to my keychain, he said, "We should really get you a taser, it's a little more reliable in the rain."

He seemed genuinely sweet.

In another life, maybe I would let this man in.

I shook my head against the temptation and turned back to the van. "I'm sorry, I have to go."

"Are you going to be okay driving home?" He asked.

"I'm not dizzy anymore." The episode was basically over —it had come on just long enough to wreck my life.

"Okay, be careful," he said.

As I got into my car, he added, "Call me if you need anything."

My face screwed up in confusion as I watched him jog through the rain back to the restaurant.

I let out a sigh and looked down at the fold of cash in my hand. When I opened it up, I found a $50 bill, wrapped around a slip of paper with a phone number and 'Captain Jeff Miller' written on it.

Oh, that's what he meant.

Well, I wouldn't be calling him. My entire life revolved around taking care of Lyric and trying to get into the Kansas

City Art Institute on a full scholarship. It was why I had moved us here two years ago. I had no intention of trusting anyone enough for even a casual relationship. My sister's safety was too important.

Shivering from the cold, I tossed the slip of paper into the door pocket that held my trash and shoved the $50 into my pocket. Then I cranked up the heat and drove home.

I parked the van outside of the shabby apartment building. Still chilled in my bones and not ready to face the rain again, I let my head fall back against the seat with the heat blasting over me. *Maybe I could sell some things to pay rent this month.* I mentally scanned the meager apartment that housed everything Lyric and I owned. There was little that was even remotely valuable. Our phones weren't that nice, but I also considered them a safety precaution. Being without them wasn't an option. My mind landed on the old, refurbished laptop I'd hidden in the back of my closet—a gift I'd saved for almost an entire year to buy, because I wanted Lyric's sixteenth birthday to be special.

I slammed my palms into the steering wheel. What was the point of my trying to get into the Art Institute when I couldn't even afford to give Lyric a birthday gift? It was selfish do something that didn't provide for us. Why had I even considered it? *Will I ever be able to do something that I want to do?*

"Not while I'm taking care of my sister." I sighed and shook my head. "No. Don't think like that Astrid." *Protecting Lyric is what I want to do.*

· · ·

I turned off the car and jumped out of the van into the pelting rain, shivering as I ran. I'd almost made it to the building when I heard the familiar screech of an angry cat.

Ope... is that?

Pausing, I looked over in the bushes and spotted the little gray tabby. He appeared as miserable as I felt. Soaked to the skin, he looked offended at the very existence of the rain. I frowned at the mud between me and the cat. I couldn't just leave him there.

I picked my way through the mire and scooped up the shivering little cat.

"Hey there, McTabby. Did Mrs. Norton let you out again?"

The cat continued to complain as I walked him over to the door. When we finally got inside, he rubbed his wet face on my chin and purred. His abnormally short tail flicked back and forth.

"What a pair we make," I said.

The cat sniffed at the pork in my hair and began to taste it. "Ope!" I laughed a little. "You always know when there's food, don't you?" I adjusted him in my arms as I walked.

"I guess it's good I brought a sample for you today since I won't be able to bring you leftovers anymore."

It took a couple of knocks on the door. Mrs. Norton finally answered. The door only opened a couple of inches before it hit her walker.

"Oh, for Pete's sake." The old woman's grumbling came from the other side of the door as she struggled to open it the rest of the way.

"It's me, Mrs. Norton." I resisted the urge to wrinkle my

nose at the reek of potpourri and ammonia coming from her apartment. "I found McTabby stuck outside again."

Mrs. Norton finally won the battle of door versus walker, breathing hard from the effort. Her lined face went from a scowl to a smile when she saw her cat. "Well, I'll be! I called and called for him—it's his suppertime."

"Well, I'm sure he's glad to be back home then!" I set the cat down. He trotted over and rubbed against Mrs. Norton's ankle affectionately.

"He's so cold and wet!" she said.

Mrs. Norton looked up from the cat and seemed to notice me for the first time. Her wrinkles deepened with disapproval. "Aren't you taking care of yourself dear? You look unkempt."

Here we go...

I worked to keep a pleasant smile on my 'unkempt' face. "Yep, it's just pouring rain out there."

Eager for clean, dry clothes, I carefully escaped the conversation about my appearance and wished her well before taking the stairs two at a time to get to my apartment.

Olive green paint peeled in places from my apartment door, revealing a faded pink color underneath. As I put the key in the lock, I straightened the number 5—a pointless exercise. It always drooped back down the doorframe again as though the building itself were stripped of its pride.

Lyric's witch bells jingled softly on the door when I opened it. My sister didn't seem to notice, as she and Tyler were on the other side of our barren apartment at the small kitchen table. They were bent over Tyler's sticker-covered laptop. I smiled at the scene. It never surprised me to find the neighbor boy here. His red hair and freckled face had been part of the landscape of our apartment since we'd moved in down the hall from him. He practically worshiped Lyric, and I could understand why. Her delicate features were a perfect match to her brave heart and beautiful soul.

"What shenanigans are happening here?" I said, alerting them to my presence.

Lyric's head came up. Her distinct silver eyes widened in horror, and she smacked Tyler's arm, causing him to look up as well.

"Whoa! Is that blood?" Tyler asked.

"Astrid, what happened to you?!" Lyric said.

"What?" Then I remembered the barbecue in my hair. "Oh! No, it's just burnt ends." I kicked off my shoes and dropped my bag on the faded brown carpet that had probably seen two decades of apartment life.

"It looks like you got in a fight!" Lyric touched her own cheek, mirroring the place where my face had met the swinging door when I'd passed out.

I shrugged. "Oh, I just fell and kind of ate the door as I went."

"Ouch! Is that why you're home so early?"

"Yep." No point getting into the details. I walked to the freezer and grabbed a bag of peas for my cheek. "So what are you two working on over there?" I asked.

"Editing," Tyler said, his attention back on the laptop.

"Astrid! You have to see the video we uploaded to my channel last week!" Lyric pushed back from the table excitedly, and Tyler jumped up to help her maneuver her wheelchair around.

"It's already gotten so many views!" he said.

Lyric being in her chair meant that she'd had a bad day physically, with her chronic fatigue syndrome. She never let it bridle her spirit, which I admired. Seeing her in her chair always got me extra protective. "Lyric, I wish you wouldn't exhaust yourself working on these projects."

"It's worth it. People are finally going to understand and start taking better care of the earth. Right Tyler?" She looked up at her best friend.

He put a hand on his chest with theatrical gravity. "It is my totally unbiased and almost professional opinion that if anyone can change the world, it's L."

She elbowed his arm playfully. She was oblivious to how smitten that boy was with her.

I smiled. "Well, can I look at your project later? I really need a shower."

"That's probably for the best." She wheeled her chair backwards away from me a little, wrinkling her nose. "I can *really* smell you."

I laughed and headed for the promise of warm, dry clothes.

Two

I was still cold after my shower, so I wrapped my long, dark hair into a ratty towel on my head and shrugged on my oversized hoodie—a soft, warm thrift store find. Lyric had urged me to choose something more flattering. 'Confidence combined with the right outfit can take a girl places,' she had told me for maybe the hundredth time.

As usual, I'd told her that I'd rather be warm and comfortable than go anywhere. Just one of the many ways my sister and I were completely different. I sighed in comfort as the warmth of the fleece hugged my body.

I headed for the kitchen to start making some rice and a simple sauce for dinner. The tiny apartment kitchen wasn't great for cooking. The dilapidated stove didn't work. Our landlord had provided us a hotplate rather than repair or replace the stove, and I'd gotten a rice cooker at the thrift store a while ago. Using small appliances in the kitchen was a risky move—I assumed because the wiring was as sketchy as the rest of the building. If the fridge motor kicked on while using the hotplate, it would trip the breaker. Strategic plug swapping was the only way to guarantee success. Of course, we had to be vigilant about plugging the fridge back in after the cooking was done so the contents would stay cold. It was all an inconvenient system that we had perfected over the two years of living in this place.

I moved the container of succulents that Lyric grew on the counter to make room for dinner prep. My sister was set on 'healing the earth, one plant at a time.' I didn't personally understand how having plants on the only two feet of counter we had in the kitchen would help save the world, but they made Lyric happy, and I couldn't argue with that.

I measured the last of our rice into the cooker. It was past time to do some grocery shopping. I thought of the $50 in the pocket of my dirty work jeans.

I'll spend my tip money on groceries and figure out the rent after that.

Not knowing where money would come from soon had me thinking about finding another job. "Hey Tyler, could I use your laptop after dinner?" Applying online was more efficient than going around in person.

"Sure, I can leave it here for you."

When dinner was mostly ready, I began clearing my art supplies off the small table. The painting I'd been working on —a child and his mom, laughing and holding on to each other as they ice skated at Crown Center—made me smile. I felt proud of how I had captured the joy in the little boy's brown eyes. My best work so far.

My smile vanished when I noticed dried oatmeal spilled

on the corner where I'd worked to get the ice to shine just right. Irritation flashed through me.

"What the heck? There's food on this!"

Lyric and Tyler both looked up from the laptop at the other end of the table. "I'm sorry," she said. "I can clean it off."

"Don't. I'll take care of it." I clenched my teeth and began carefully pulling the dried bits off. "I just wish you guys wouldn't eat next to my art."

"It's the kitchen table." There was a bit of edginess in her tone. "Where else are we supposed to eat?"

"It's also my art table."

The food was coming off, but it was taking some of the paint with it. I wanted to scream. I tried so hard to never waste paint and even still I was running low. There was no way I could get more any time soon. It was the cherry on my bad-day sundae.

"This piece was important to me!"

Good thing I already submitted my application portfolio.

Tyler stood and shoved his hands in his pockets. "It was my fault. I'm sorry." He rocked on his feet. "I meant to clean it up right away."

His fault or not, he would have taken the heat for Lyric. It was sweet but didn't help my mood. I wanted to just talk to Lyric about boundaries, sister-to-sister, without feeling like I was outnumbered. I took a breath and tried to tamp down my frustration, but my words still came out icy. "Tyler, I think it's time for you to go home for the night."

Lyric grabbed Tyler's arm. "No! Stay! It's movie night."

"Lyric," Tyler spoke before I had a chance to respond.

His blue eyes looked into her silver ones with earnest. "I'd slay a dragon for you—but I am not crossing Astrid."

I rolled my eyes, not in the mood for his banter.

"Astrid!" She turned scolding silver eyes on me. "You can't just kick him out because you're mad at me."

Tyler touched Lyric's arm and said, "I've gotta go anyway. My stepdad texted me a while ago, threatening to smash my desktop set-up if I didn't have dinner ready when he got home."

"You're going to actually cook for that jerk?" Lyric said.

"No. I'm going to go make sure all my tech is hidden where he can't find it before I head out to do some work on my bike."

Lyric scrunched up her nose. "There's no way that motorcycle needs any work."

"Hey, I've still gotta check on her, or she might think I have another woman." Tyler winked and headed for the door.

He didn't take his laptop with him—apparently he remembered his promise to let me borrow it. I felt like a jerk.

It had taken me a couple of months to warm up to the idea of a teenage boy stepping foot in our house. But he was a good kid.

"Tyler," I called after him, "if you need a place to keep your computers safe, you can bring them over here for a while."

"Thanks Astrid. I might just take you up on that offer," he said before ducking out of the apartment.

I put my painting in my room and returned to the kitchen. I had a whole slew of things I wanted to say.

Without meaning to, I led with, "Lyric, I know it's hard being stuck in this apartment all the time, but—"

"Actually, you don't know," she cut in, gesturing with her hands. "You get to leave every day while I'm trapped here."

The change in direction for the conversation was standard procedure. We'd had this argument more times than I could count.

Impatient, I responded as usual. "You know this is how it has to be."

"For how long?" Lyric folded her arms. "It's been five years since Mom died."

"You know I don't have an answer to that." I looked down. My toes fiddled with the hole in my sock.

"She told you to keep me hidden," Lyric said. "But maybe she only meant for a little while." She threw her hands up in frustration. "You don't even know!"

"Neither do you." I pointed at myself for emphasis, "and I'm still in charge."

"What am I even hiding from at this point?!" She gestured around the room that was empty of threats. "I just want to be a normal teenager and do normal things!"

"You *are* normal Lyric—" My heart ached.

I never meant for her to feel this way.

"If I was normal," she scoffed, "you would let me go to public school with Tyler."

We both knew I wasn't going to do that.

"Even if I let you go to public school, you would not be going anywhere on a motorcycle."

Lyric scowled. "Just because you're afraid of everything and everyone doesn't make it all dangerous."

I folded my arms and smirked. I had data to back me up on this point. "Hundreds of fatalities support my being against motorcycles."

"Well, what about school?" She thrust her chin forward, defiant. "Why can't I go to high school?"

I sighed and let my arms drop. "There are lots of reasons, Lyric. We've been over this."

There was no winning this argument. It was always circular, and it always sucked.

"You're so paranoid about everything," she whispered. "You don't even let me live life." She slumped against the back of her wheelchair, looking defeated.

My anger drained away.

She was right. I didn't let her do almost anything.

I had taken up Mom's torch after she had died and kept us on the move, as she had. Only spending a few months at a time in any given town. ...Hiding from most human interaction.

I didn't know what mom was afraid of. The accident hadn't left much time for explanations, so I was paranoid about everyone and everything. 'Never let anyone get close to us' had been my motto for almost five years.

Now here we were, settling down in Kansas City so that I could pursue my dream of the art institute. It felt risky. But I'd wanted to it do since I was a kid, and we'd stopped at a rest stop in Missouri on our way to whatever remote location Mom was taking us to next. I'd found a brochure for the art institute. The school looked like a brick mansion, and my ten-year-old heart had come alive with the idea of belonging there someday. I was so close to making it happen.

Lyric was still under lockdown.

But what else could I do? Letting her go out was dangerous, especially now that we were staying in one place for a while. Something bad could happen to her. She was already so fragile.

I was glad she had found a friend in Tyler. She deserved happiness more than I did.

"I'm sorry," I said. "I wish I could fix things, but I don't know how."

"Let me go to school. Or let me put my face in my videos." She gave me a challenging look.

"You know I can't do that, L."

She shook her head. "You mean you won't."

"We'll figure something out, okay?" I said, hoping to restore the peace. "For now, let's eat dinner."

I helped her roll her chair back to the table.

We ate in silence for a while.

Finally, Lyric said, "Tyler didn't even eat breakfast here this morning."

"Huh?"

"It was me who spilled on your painting."

I recognized Lyric's peace offering.

I returned her gesture with a playful tone. "That explains only one dirty bowl in the sink."

The tension dissipated, and we smiled at each other.

"I'll be more careful," she said. "I promise."

I shrugged. "I shouldn't have left it on the table. It was my fault as much as anyone's."

"That painting was really good," she said. "I'm sure it's going to get you the scholarship."

"I hope so." I hadn't wanted anything this much as long as I could remember.

"I believe in you." Her tone was full of genuine admiration.

She was the most amazing person in the whole world.

"I love you," I said.

Lyric leaned forward playfully. "Ditto a million." It had been her 'I love you' to me since she was five years old and somehow felt more special because it was just ours.

"I feel kind of bad for the kid," I said to Lyric as I stood to clear the dishes after dinner.

"Who? Tyler?" She rolled her chair into the kitchen behind me.

"Yeah."

"He's 17—not really a kid," Lyric said. "But why do you feel bad for him?"

"He's completely in love with you. And who could blame him—look at you!" I gestured to her.

She waved me off. "He knows I'm not into him. We're best friends."

"I know. And I'm glad you have him."

She nudged my arm. "*We* have him."

I smiled. "Hey, why don't you tell him to come back after he visits his bike?"

"Yeah?"

"Movie night must go on." I raised my fist in a gesture of playful triumph.

Lyric hugged me around my waist. The only time she was shorter than me was when she used her chair. Her genes were quite the opposite of mine. Where my hair was dark, hers was fair. Where I was short, she was tall.

My thoughts were interrupted by Tyler coming through the door carrying a box overflowing with computer parts. Lyric and he decided on the best place to put his things. By the time I finished washing dishes, Tyler had all of his equipment gathered in the corner of our mostly empty living room. It had taken several trips for him to bring over years' worth of carefully procured equipment, and now he was back for movie night.

"You guys ready for movie night?" Tyler rubbed his hands together and smiled, adding in a little eyebrow waggle.

Months ago, in a drunken rage, Tyler's stepdad cracked the screen of their TV in the top corner. After two days, he'd sobered up and spent their rent money on a new one. Tyler had been told to take their old one to the dumpster, but he'd snuck it into our apartment instead. There it sat—a lone trophy on the floor of a living room lined with nothing but a few plants. That night, Tyler had hacked the Wi-Fi from the next apartment and logged the TV into his streaming service. Friday night movie night had been born, and he and Lyric hadn't missed one since. The fact that the corner of the TV had a crack was only a slight distraction for us, and movie night didn't suffer for it.

As custom dictated, we dragged a mattress from the single bedroom to the living room, and all three of us piled on.

"You two pick the movie. I'll make some popcorn," I said, heading into the kitchen.

Halfway through heating the oil in the pan, the fridge motor kicked on and all the lights went out.

"On it!" Tyler called from the other room before I even moved.

I grumbled at myself for forgetting to unplug the fridge before using the hotplate. Once the lights were back on, I swapped the plugs and added the kernels to the oil.

"Looks like you're popping more than popcorn in here," Tyler said with finger guns in my direction as he passed by me on his way to the living room.

I rolled my eyes and smiled at his terrible pun, then shooed him out of the kitchen.

Before he disappeared around the corner, he turned back. "Hey! Wanna hear a popcorn joke?" Then added, "Nah, it's too corny." His hand flew to his mouth in mock surprise. "Ope! That popped out of nowhere."

"Oh. My. Word. Make it stop." I threw a popcorn kernel at him. He laughed, ducking behind the doorway.

The smell of popcorn began to fill the kitchen, and Lyric's unrestrained laughter floated in as Tyler said something else I didn't hear. My sister laughed so readily. If only I wasn't so boring and serious. I shook my head. *Someone has to be the responsible one.*

Lyric fell asleep during the movie. I didn't want to wake her to move the mattress, so she was there for the night. She looked so young.

I smoothed her hair, remembering the day my mom brought Lyric home. Before that, it had been just me and mom for my first seven years. We'd moved around so much that I didn't even have time to make friends. I'd been in my room while Mom was out doing a tarot reading for a client. She came home having adopted a silver-eyed baby. My mom had placed Lyric in my arms and said that the universe had brought me a sister. I couldn't have been more thrilled.

I wasn't ready to sleep yet, so after Tyler left, I wrapped myself in a big blanket and sat down at the table with his laptop to do some job searching.

The screen woke to the page it was on when Lyric had closed it earlier. When I saw what she had been working on, my stomach dropped.

My sister's unearthly silver eyes stared back at me from her latest video, sending chills down my spine.

People have watched this video.

Lyric had been making videos for her 'Heal the Earth' channel for a while and they'd gone from mediocre and obscure to quite good. But until now, every video had followed our late Mom's number one Stone-house-rule.

Absolutely no pictures of us online. No exceptions.

My breathing felt shaky and my heart was pounding.

Will we have to move again?

Seeing Lyric's face on the screen triggered a memory from when I was about nine. I'd often been in charge of taking care of my baby sister. But if Mom had to work for too long or be too far away, an old wrinkly woman with warm eyes would come over to babysit us. I called her Gran, and I adored her. She read to us, and she sometimes baked cookies, something Mom never did. No one in the world gave better hugs than Gran. When she tucked me in at night, she would say, "Goodnight, Pumpkin Bear."

One day, Gran dressed us all up and took us to a photography studio, where she got a picture of Lyric and me printed and framed to surprise our mom.

When Mom had opened the gift, instead of being happy,

she'd looked angry. So many years later, I realize she'd been terrified.

That night, she'd packed two bags, loaded us into the car, and we drove for what seemed like days before we found a new home. Lyric was too young to understand, but I wasn't. We would never get to see Gran again.

I glanced over at my sleeping sister.

She's always been so fragile. That was really hard on Mom.

All my life I'd been given a steady stream of lectures from Mom on how to blend in and be careful. And after the Gran debacle, it took my mom years before she loosened up about pictures. After Mom died, I had gotten Lyric a phone with an actual good camera on it. She had been thrilled. She had sworn to follow Mom's rules, even though Mom was gone. I was responsible for her safety now. If anything happened, it would be my fault.

Watching the way Lyric moved and spoke in this video was pretty mesmerizing. Her thoughts were compelling and her passion for the earth inspired me as I watched it.

Lyric is really proud of this project. I wish I'd paid more attention to what she was working on instead of being so caught up with my own stuff. I clicked the play button to watch it again.

She really could *change the world.*

When the video finished for the second time, I let the mouse hover over the 'un-publish' button.

It's what Mom would have wanted me to do, no question.

But it seemed like a huge overstep. I bit my bottom lip in deliberation.

Lyric worked so hard on this project and she's right, it really is good.

I tapped the table a few times.

Maybe Mom had needed to lighten up.

I sighed.

Maybe Mom had known things I don't.

In the end, I decided it wouldn't do any more damage to leave the video published until morning. Then I could just talk to Lyric about it and have her take it down.

Promising myself I would job search in the morning, I closed the laptop and headed to my room.

THREE

I t was still dark outside when I woke the next morning from a graphic nightmare in which everything I touched turned to ash. I didn't feel much like trying to go back to sleep. The first signs of a migraine were knocking on my skull, and I massaged my temples.

I need coffee.

I pulled on my black yoga pants and a crop top with long sleeves.

After brewing myself some instant coffee, I decided to get groceries so that breakfast would be available when Lyric woke.

Maybe it'll soften the blow of the video conversation.

I really wanted to avoid another argument.

Counting my tip money from the night before, I calculated which items I could afford and what would last us the longest. Then I scribbled a note for Lyric to tell her where I'd gone.

The deadbolt clicked softly into place. I double checked the handle was locked as well before I headed for the van.

The humidity in the air made my skin feel sticky and the chilly air feel even cooler. *I regret my decision to leave without a jacket.*

After paying for the groceries, I felt a little proud of myself. I had gotten pretty good at shopping on a tight budget over the years, but despite this having been an extra frugal trip, I was confident that we would not starve for at least two weeks.

As I pushed my cart of groceries towards the door I'd come in, a flier on the "Have You Seen Me?" board caught my eye. I usually breezed past it, but the face on this particular ad stopped me in my tracks.

I stepped up to get a closer look at the girl. My mouth hung open in horror. She looked eerily like Lyric in the age-progressed photo. My head swam. *This can't be Lyric, it's just the strange silver eyes that make this girl look like her.*

But even as my mind tried to justify it, I couldn't deny that it was more than the eyes that looked like hers. The heart-shaped face, the slim nose, the way her right eyebrow peaked slightly higher than the left.

It's a computer age-progressed photo. This girl probably doesn't really look like Lyric in real life.

I glanced around. It was still early, so the store was mostly empty, except for a few workers who weren't paying any attention to me.

Snatching the flier off of the corkboard, I shoved it in a bag of groceries between the flour and the jar of peanut butter. Then I headed for the van.

· · ·

After loading the groceries into the side door, I hopped into the driver's seat just as rain started dotting the windshield. I ignored the headache that was coming on strong, and I twisted around to dig the flyer out of the bag in the back seat. My heart hammered as I examined the flier carefully. The picture that looked like Lyric, really looked like Lyric. The second picture was of an infant.

Lyric Smith.

I felt queasy. *Lyric is* not *a common name.*

Last seen in Maryland.

Isn't that where we lived when we adopted Lyric?

I mentally calculated from the 'date missing'—fifteen years ago.

Not possible. I shook my head.

Reward for any information.

Is this why Mom was so paranoid?

I felt sick to my stomach and utterly alone in the world.

Mom, what did you do?

Who could I even talk to about this? What did it all mean?

There had to be an explanation that made sense. Mom had been an amazing person. Her entire world had revolved around me and Lyric.

What if it was all a lie?

I went over the details of Lyric's arrival in my mind, searching for clues or strange behavior. A hazy picture formed in my memory. Mom telling me, "It's a game Astrid. Don't peek, no matter what you hear." Like any self-respecting 7-year-old, I had peeked. A man, bloody and bruised. A baby crying. Angry words that I didn't quite hear.

I hadn't thought about that night in so long, I wasn't sure if it was a memory or a dream.

I shook my head. My migraine spiking. I rubbed a thumb over the amber stone in my leather bracelet cuff.

What if my mom was a kidnapper?

No. She was a good person. She loved us.

My head was pounding. I rummaged in my bag and found my medicine.

I tossed the flier onto the passenger seat and rubbed my temples, willing myself to forget about the whole thing.

The flier glared at me.

Groaning in frustration, I grabbed the paper, ripped it in half, and crumpled it into a ball. I tossed it behind me and drove home.

I had enough to worry about without obsessing over this stupid flier.

Once I got home, I grabbed all the groceries in one big load and jogged through the light rain into the apartment building. As I ascended the stairs, I rehearsed different ways that I could broach the topic of Lyric taking her video down. I didn't want my stress to make this conversation any worse.

Just be casual about it.

I found my house key on the ring and jiggled it into the lock. I didn't get it all the way in before Lyric opened the door wide, grinning at me—no wheelchair in sight. "Good morning!"

I smiled back. "You're awake."

"It's such a beautiful morning!" She grabbed a couple of bags from me.

I looked at her, confused. "It's gray and raining out there."

She ignored me and walked into the kitchen.

"Looks like you're feeling pretty strong today." I gestured to her empty wheelchair across the livingroom.

"I feel like I could do anything today." She spun in a little circle.

I raised my eyebrows. "What's got you in such a good mood?"

We both started putting the groceries away.

"My newest video is getting tons of hits!" She bounced a bit with each word.

I closed my eyes. My mission to casually have her take that video down would not go well.

"Oh?" I put the carton of eggs into the fridge as Lyric kept talking.

"Oh my gosh Astrid, what if it goes viral!" She clasped her hands. "I'm so excited!"

I bit my lower lip and held my breath.

Deciding on the quick, straightforward approach, I turned to face her. "I think you need to redo that video. You have your face in it."

"You watched it?" She looked upset.

"I thought you wanted me to see it." I smiled trying to recover. "It was amazing!"

She folded her arms. "Then you know why I'm not taking it down."

I picked up the flour and put it in the cabinet. "But you know Mom's number one rule."

"Mom is gone." Lyric's tone was firm. "I'm done following her rules."

"They're also my rules." I tried to sound gentle and understanding, but it came out condescending. The flier this morning had thrown me, and I couldn't seem to recover.

"I'm almost sixteen." Lyric straightened. "Age of emancipation in Missouri, so I can do what I want."

"I hate to tell you this," my tone dripped with satisfaction, "but you can't emancipate unless you're supporting yourself financially."

"Then that's what I'll do." She shrugged.

I looked at her flatly. "You can't be serious."

I'm glad I didn't tell her about losing my job. She might think it's another reason for mutiny.

"Astrid, you are so controlling, just like Mom was." She turned to walk away. "I'm not going to live like this anymore."

Her words hurt.

My migraine was dizzying despite the medication.

"How am I supposed to protect you when you're constantly fighting against me?" I yelled after her.

I was making a mess of everything.

If Lyric goes to live on her own, how will I take care of her?

How am I supposed to take care of her now with no job?

Things had gone so wrong.

I escaped to my room to calm down.

I laid on my bed, emotionally drained. Still morning and already I felt like I wanted the day to be over. Uncomfortably cold, I pulled the blankets over me and buried my face in the pillow. The amber stone in my bracelet anchored me as I stroked its smooth surface. Mom had given me the cuff when I was little. It had been an arm band until I'd grown into it.

"It once belonged to your grandmother, a woman with great courage and power." She had told me the story so many times. "Anytime you wear it you will have her strength to guide you."

My thoughts were interrupted when the door to the bedroom banged against the wall as Lyric barged in.

"What is this?" She demanded.

I sat up to face her, my words dying in my throat when I saw what she held up. Wrinkled and torn in two, but still very much readable. The "Have You Seen Me?" flier with the picture that resembled so closely the face of the girl holding it.

"Where did you get that?"

"From a grocery bag." She shook the flier for emphasis. "Why am I on this flier?"

I couldn't find a response.

"Was I kidnapped?" Her eyes were filling with tears.

"No!" I stood up and tried to take the flier, but she moved it out of my reach.

"Is this why I'm not allowed to go anywhere or do anything?"

I looked up at her beautiful face, now full of betrayal. My shoulders drooped. "I don't know."

"What do you mean you don't know?" She took a step back. "You're saying I *might* have been kidnapped?"

The pain on her face tore at my heart. Wanting to comfort her, but also wanting to defend our mom, I deflected. "I just saw that flier this morning at the store. I don't know what it means. Mom isn't here to ask her about it."

"Is this why we keep moving? So my real family won't find me?"

"Lyric, I am your real family. I don't know what the flier means."

"How can you say you don't know what it means?" She glanced at the flier before shoving it towards my face. "There's not much else it *can* mean!"

My sister stormed off with the flier in hand and locked herself in the bathroom.

Shaking with stress and nauseous from the pain of the migraine, I paced in the hall, wearing my thumb raw with rubbing my cuff—If ever I had needed guidance, it was now. I was torn between giving her space and demanding she come out so we could deal with this together.

Through the door, I could hear Lyric's muffled voice, "Hi, I think I have information on a missing person. The case number is—"

Oh my god!

I pounded on the bathroom door. "Lyric, hang up the phone! We have to talk about this!"

We had one of those bathroom locks that could be picked with a hairpin in the outside hole. I ran into my room scouring my dresser for a hairpin. When I finally located one I rushed back into the hall, stubbing my toe on the door frame and crying out a curse. My hands were shaking so picking the lock took twice as long as it should have. I could hear her talking to the person on the phone the whole time. When I finally burst into the room, she flashed me a defiant look as she hit the end call button. My blood was boiling. "What did you do?"

"I did what you're supposed to do when you're kidnapped." She stuck her chin out. "I called for help."

"Lyric!" I pressed my hands to either side of my pulsing head. "We should have talked about it and made a decision together."

She shook her head. "It's not your decision to make. I'm the person on this poster."

Lyric put her phone in her back pocket with a finality that said she felt powerful. But as she walked past me and through the hall, I noticed she used the wall for support. Clearly, she would need her chair soon, despite how good she'd felt this morning.

"I'm going to Tyler's." She didn't look back as she left the apartment.

My thoughts were frantic.

What would all of this mean?

Will someone come for her?

Should we pack up and leave tonight?

Would Lyric even go if I asked her?

I decided to go on a run to clear my head. I didn't bother stretching, just desperately stumbled down the steps and out of the building. Light rain tickled my face—I didn't care. I just ran. I tried not to think about how we might need to move again, or how I might have to give up my dream of the Art Institute. I just ran. I tried not to think about how Lyric hated me and how I could lose her forever. I just ran.

. . .

I didn't know how long I was gone. I'd left my phone somewhere at home in my desperation to escape the apartment. I hoped Lyric would let me in if she was home, because I hadn't even taken my keys with me.

My soaked shoes squeaked as I walked. The drizzle had stopped, and the sun was out, but my feet felt pruney. When I looked up at my apartment door, I froze. The jam was splintered and broken, and the door hung by one hinge.

A break-in. Had we been robbed?

What could they have taken?

Heart thumping in my chest, I inched the door open and tilted my ear closer to listen. Silence came from inside. I opened the door further and called out, "Lyric?"

No answer.

Maybe she's still at Tyler's.

It didn't take me long to look through every room. She wasn't there. Her wheelchair sat near the mattress, still on the living room floor.

My chest constricted.

I tamped down my fear. *She's probably at Tyler's.*

I noticed a few drops of greenish oil or paint on the floor. Did they break in for art supplies? That didn't make any sense.

I didn't bother looking for what the intruders might have taken—we had little worth stealing. But I prayed Lyric had still been at Tyler's when the break-in happened.

My fist pounded on the door of Tyler's apartment more forcefully than I had intended.

Chill out, she's going to be here.

When it took too long to answer, I knocked again.

If she's over here, why aren't they answering the door?

The door opened just enough to make the chain on the inside lock pull tight. The man's narrow eyes that appeared in the crack were bloodshot and full of anger. It gave me an instant sense of why Tyler hated this man. "What do you want?"

"Is my sister here?"

"Why the hell would your sister be here?"

"She said she was coming here."

Panic rose in my chest.

She has to be here. She wouldn't go anywhere else! "Can I talk to Tyler?"

"He and his little girlfriend went somewhere together."

He slammed the door as hard as seemed possible with only the few inches of swing.

They went somewhere together.

On his motorcycle, no doubt. My sister was so grounded.

The thought irritated me as much as it was comforting— at least Lyric hadn't been home when the break-in happened. I tried calling her phone. No answer. She was probably still mad at me.

Still, I paced the floor wondering where she was. I used my phone to find the location of Lyric's phone. That feature the main reason I deemed it necessary to have these things. In case of separation. It felt a little like an overstep, tracking her when she clearly wanted some space. But it would comfort me to know for sure where she was.

Lyric's little dot popped up on the map near the Berkley River Front, downtown Kansas City.

What are they doing there?

It's not where I would have expected them to go.

I stopped at the apartment to grab my keys before heading for the van.

I'm just going to check on them. I don't care if Lyric thinks I'm overprotective.

The break-in at our apartment had my nerves on edge, and I didn't like Lyric being gone and mad at me.

I would just drive by.

Maybe they won't notice me.

The ignition simply clicked without turning over. I was going to be stuck waiting here for Lyric to cool off and come home. I tried turning the key several more times, but the van wouldn't start.

The break-in might be a good excuse to convince Lyric to move somewhere new.

Knowing that someone had just barged into our apartment was completely unsettling.

I studied the shabby building that had been home for longer than any other place in my life. It seemed kind of sad to leave, but it no longer felt safe to me. I narrowed my eyes at the motorcycle parked just across the lot.

Tyler's motorcycle.

What is that doing here?

Downtown was not within walking distance, and Tyler didn't have any other transportation. Something did not add up.

I tried calling Lyric's phone again. Still no answer. I sent her a text that just said, "Call me!"

Then checked on her location again. Still near the Berkley River Front.

Dread weighed my body down. After the break-in at the

apartment, I had to see with my own eyes that Lyric was safe. I sprinted back up the stairs and pounded on Tyler's apartment door once again.

This time, Tyler's mother opened the door, her hair a mess. "Astrid?" She looked at me in surprise. "What are you thinking? My husband is trying to sleep. Do you want us all murdered?"

"I'm so sorry," I said, not missing a beat. "We have car trouble and Tyler had said that I could borrow his bike today. I forgot to get the keys from him last night, so I just need to grab them quick. I'm running late." It was hard to keep my foot from tapping with impatience.

The woman looked at me with narrowed eyes and then closed the door. I waited a beat and then made to knock again, but just as I lifted my fist to the door, I heard the chain inside rattle and Tyler's mom opened the door wider than before. She held out a small key chain with a single key on it —the key to the thing that Tyler loved more than anything in the world, except maybe Lyric. I thanked her as I grabbed the key and tried not to seem too eager. Then she handed me his helmet. "Be careful. God knows I hate that thing. It's so dangerous."

"I know, I'll be careful."

After strapping on the helmet, I straddled the bike. My toes barely reached the ground, and only on one side at a time.

This is a terrible idea.

But despite all my better instincts, I forged ahead. "I'm sorry, Tyler." I said, "I'll bring it back."

As soon as I put the key into the ignition, I realized that

this was not like driving a car. I tried a few things unsuccessfully, before pulling out my phone and doing a quick search. The minutes that ticked by while I gave myself a crash course in starting and driving a bike felt like an eternity. After following the online instructions for the bike, its engine rumbled beneath me.

Yes!

Victorious in at least getting the thing started, I moved to the next steps, which involved gear shifting—an obnoxious complication that I felt I could have done without.

Even with all of my new knowledge, figuring out how to drive the bike proved disastrous at first. I stalled out a few times and tipped it over, skinning my inner calf.

Why do they even make these things?

Once I got going, I was shaking. My first few turns were wobbly and wide. I almost lost my balance and realized that in order to stay upright, I would need to drive faster. Fear gripped my chest as I urged the bike forward. The terror became almost exhilarating as I picked up speed, but the whole stopping part loomed in my future like a dreadful promise.

I prayed I could just get to Lyric and that everything would, in fact, prove to be fine.

I'm just being paranoid.

Lyric is safe.

I told myself that the dread in my gut was just a combination of the break-in at home, and the bike I was on, careening down I-35 at 60 MPH. Several cars passed on my left. The whoosh of air causing me to tense every time.

If Lyric were here, she would definitely comment on my going ten under the speed limit.

But I couldn't bring myself to let the bike go any faster.

Twenty minutes later, I pulled up under the Heart of America bridge that crosses the Missouri River. I planted my toes on the ground on the left side of the bike. The place was deserted in an eerie way. There was no trace of Lyric or Tyler. I tapped the screen to light up my phone. When I pulled up the map that had Lyric's location, I looked at it with a mixture of horror and disbelief. Lyrics dot hovered in the middle of the river.

My migraine spiked into the mother of all migraines. I tore the helmet off my head, my heart racing.

What if Lyric drowned?

The pain in my head set my stomach churning. I dropped the bike, falling to my knees to retch.

Once my stomach was decidedly empty, I was left shaking. I clutched my cuff bracelet like a lifeline.

Get it together, Astrid.

I was afraid of what I would find when I looked at the river, but I convinced myself that it was just a GPS glitch.

Lyric and Tyler are probably sitting down by the edge of the river. Maybe she dropped her phone in.

I picked myself up along with the motorcycle. In my haze of pain, I couldn't get the kickstand to go down, so I rolled the bike over to one side of the bridge and wedged the thing between some bushes. I threw the helmet into the brush next to it. Rubbing my thumb over the amber stone in my cuff, I went to get a good look at the river.

It was as if, by stepping close to the water I had passed through some unseen barrier. One moment, the river was empty. The next moment, the river was filled with a ship, shrouded in green mist. I gasped. It looked like something you might find in a pirate movie—menacing with its dark tattered sails and looming larger than physics deemed possible in the muddy river.

I took a trembling step back. The entire scene shimmered like a mirage before it vanished, and all that remained was the empty river. My gaze darted back and forth in confusion.

I slid my foot forward, tentatively following with my throbbing head to cross the invisible barrier. The ship was there again. *Maybe it's a side effect of this heinous pain in my head.*

I rubbed my temples and squeezed my eyes shut before opening them again to the same scene.

I took a shaky breath and looked around. I was alone except for the pirate ship before me. Dragging my phone from my pocket, I checked the location of Lyric's phone again. The dot still hovered in the middle of the river. To my relief and horror, it seemed to be on board this creepy vanishing ship.

My brain couldn't make sense of it.

Maybe it's some kind of haunted house?

I knew it wasn't. My gut told me there was danger. And if Lyric was on that ship, I had to find her.

FOUR

Climbing up the back end of a strange ship was never something I'd thought I would do. Now that I'd checked it off of my non-bucket list, I never need to do it again. Not to mention, the pillars between each level of this ship were creepy figurines that belonged in a horror movie. Using them as climbing holds had my already weakened stomach uneasy.

I'd opted to climb rather than use the gangplank for two reasons. First, I hadn't been able to find one. Second—and more importantly—the men, or rather the humanoid creatures, that milled about on the deck were grotesque. Their knotted features and various shades of green skin had me grossed out, but on top of that, they looked menacing. Let's just say I was keen to find Lyric without making any new friends.

When I reached the first level balcony and windows, I collapsed over the railing, muscles shaking. Trying to heavy-breathe silently, I glanced around. No one was on this balcony. I peered into the frosted glass of the nearest window.

Two creatures in the room conversed. Their mouths moved around sharp-pointed teeth and purple tongues. They mesmerized me in a petrifying way. Clearly these were not costumes.

Afraid to move, but more afraid to linger, I inched my way towards the nearest pillar and didn't draw breath until I was away from view. Then I wrapped my arms around myself. My body was cold and my head full of pain.

Why would Lyric come here?

The more I thought about it, the more worried I became. I was pretty sure Lyric didn't come here on purpose. I thought about our apartment door. Broken. Our apartment itself. Nothing of value to rob.

What if she'd been kidnapped and brought here?

But she has her phone. Kidnappers don't let you keep your phone.

I touched the cool stone in my cuff and told myself to focus. Find Lyric, and I would find answers.

I checked my phone for Lyric's location. It seemed like she was a little further towards the front of the ship, so I headed that direction.

I spent some time sneaking around. The wood floor was grimy and worn. I stumbled across some sort of supply room filled with crates. It smelled like wet dog, and there was a group of goblins arguing on the far side of the room. Their language sounded animalistic, and seeing them so close with their knobby green skin and yellow eyes made the blood drain from my face. I ducked out without being seen.

I came upon a room that smelled like rotten eggs containing two sets of unkempt bunkbeds. My already nauseous gut lurched. I escaped to the open air of the deck.

Trying more doors along this corridor produced more sleeping quarters and a few near misses with some of the goblin sailors.

I was no closer to Lyric's location. This part of the ship didn't seem to connect far enough forward. I gritted my teeth in frustration. I had to get to the next level of decks.

So, grabbing hold of the nearest goblin pillar, I climbed up to the next deck, my shaking muscles protesting the entire time. When I eased my head over the side to peek through the spindles in the railing, the stench hit me—foul mud and decay. Then I saw them—a pair of hairy green feet, inches from the railing. I ducked my head back down. Too late. The goblin started shouting something in their strange language.

I tried to climb back down, but pain erupted in my scalp. I was being pulled up by my hair. I screamed. Kicking and thrashing, I tried to get free. They had me surrounded. The first goblin didn't let go of my hair, and two more pairs of green hands grabbed at my arms. They pulled me to my feet. Several crude weapons pointed at my face. The creature in front of me, his leathery skin marked with slashing scars, growled something. His sharp, rotting teeth inches away, droplets of spit flying at my face as he spoke. I recoiled. The cold metal of a weapon touched the skin of my neck. I froze. In light of the weapons and the teeth, but mostly the weapons, I took a shaky breath and willed my panic to calm.

When I spoke, my voice trembled. "I... I don't understand what you're saying." The goblins glanced at each other before focusing back on me. Their expressions didn't change.

"I'm just here to find my sister."

The goblin in front of me growled, but I pressed on. "If I

can just grab her, we'll get out of your hair..." I looked up at the bald heads of the creatures glowering at me.

"I don't want any trouble. I just want my sister."

The goblin to my left spoke this time.

"I don't understand what you're saying to me," I said.

The creatures grunted and growled at each other. Then the one on my left lumbered away, leaving two weapons at my throat instead of three.

He was only gone a short time before he came back with another goblin. The new guy had circular, patterned tattoos around his eyes.

Tattoo guy said nothing to me. He only reached out his gnarly green hand and touched my forehead with three long dirty nails. The touch sent a shock surging through my gut. My insides felt like they were being ripped out. I don't know if I screamed before I passed out.

"Astrid... Astrid? Wake up Astrid!"

My eyes fluttered open to see Lyric's face above me. Inhaling sharply, I tried to sit up and swayed a bit.

Lyric threw her arms around me. "Astrid! Oh thank god. I thought you'd never wake up!"

"Where are we?" My voice sounded hoarse, and my mouth felt like cotton. My migraine was gone, but that's where the good news ended.

"We're in prison!" Lyric said.

I looked around. The space was small and filthy. The cell contained chains on the wall and a bucket in the corner. On the other side of the grimy steel bars, the rest of the room was almost as bare as the cell. There was a pair of goblins sitting at a wooden table, and a few hooks with metal contraptions on them. The entire space wasn't much bigger than an average bedroom.

As usual, when anxiety spiked, my hand went to the cuff on my arm to find comfort in my mother's stone.

It was gone.

The cuff that I had worn every day of my life, for as long as I could remember, had been stripped from me.

Panic rose in my chest.

"Astrid, it was so scary." Lyric was practically in tears. It pulled me back to the present. "These nasty men broke down the apartment door."

"I can't believe I let this happen." I was talking about both the kidnapping and the missing cuff.

"I've never seen anything like it, Astrid." She spoke in a whisper. "When we got to this ship, the men didn't look human anymore." She glanced over to where the two goblins sat at a table across the room.

"You see them too, right?"

"Yeah, they look like..." I couldn't bring myself to say the word. It sounded insane.

"Trolls? Goblins?"

"Yes! And goblins aren't real."

"Whatever they are, they're real." She wrinkled her nose. "And they smell horrible."

I recounted how I'd gotten captured. My hand kept seeking my arm where the absence of my cuff was like a missing piece of myself.

"How did you know I was here?" she asked.

"I tracked your phone."

"Well, if you came to rescue me, it's not going well,

because we're both on the wrong side of the bars." She gestured around us.

The rocking of the ship beneath me caused my stomach to lurch.

"Ugh, I might puke."

Lyric helped me to the bucket in the corner of our cell and held my hair back. I wiped my mouth on the knee of my leggings.

So gross.

The guards sniggered at my being sick. I flipped them off. They went back to playing some kind of card game.

Once I had puked, I felt better, though still a little dizzy.

Lyric and I huddled together in the cell, and I hugged her. "Did they hurt you?"

"No. But you would have been proud. I fought hard and made one of them bleed."

"Good." I smiled at the thought of my gentle, fragile sister getting one of the goblins.

"Tyler fought too, and they roughed him up pretty good. It was awful."

"Oh no! I hope he's okay."

"I hope so too. They tied him up and brought him with us, but they obviously didn't put him in here with me."

Crap. How are we going to get out of this mess?

At that point, a third goblin came into the room. It was the same one with circular face tattoos that had touched my skin and made me pass out. I stood up, wanting to be ready for whatever was happening. Lyric followed suit.

The goblins exchanged a few grunts. Then one guard picked up the keys from the table where they'd been playing cards and approached the the cell. Circle tattoo guy followed close behind him.

"Get behind me," I said, pushing Lyric back.

"What are they doing?"

"I don't know, but I won't let them touch you."

When the goblins stepped into the cell, I used my two months of long-ago Hapkido training to take a fight-stance and then land a kick to the guard's groin. He didn't seem nearly as affected by that as a human man would have been. I tried to punch him in the face, but after my first attack, the goblins were more prepared. Two of them grabbed me, twisting my arms back at a painful angle. When one of them grabbed Lyric, my anger flared red-hot in my gut. She clawed at her captor's face.

They rewarded us for our efforts with manacles around our ankles and wrists.

Two feet of chain bolted us to the wall. Lyric cried and screamed. I struggled against the restraints but couldn't get close enough to touch her or fight back against our captors.

After they chained us up, the original two guards went back to sitting at the table. Rather than playing cards, they watched, smirking as the circle tattoo goblin straightened his robe and once again approached me.

I tried to bite his hand, but he grabbed my chin and squeezed. The moment my skin came into contact with his, the same shocking pain from before shot through me. I fought it in my mind. I didn't want to pass out this time. Maybe staying awake and withstanding the pain would protect Lyric from having to endure it next. I gritted my teeth against the scream of agony that escaped anyway.

The pain tore at me, taking part of my soul with it. After

what seemed like a long time, the tattooed goblin let go. He smiled at me and gently patted my cheek. The triumph in his eyes another violation. He turned and walked away. To my relief, he didn't even spare a glance at Lyric.

After he left, I allowed my shaking body to slump back against the wall. How a single touch could torture me in such a profound way, I wasn't sure, but I felt completely bare. My chin trembled, betraying the façade of bravery I wore. I held the tears back and avoided Lyric's gaze. Though she called my name over and over again, I didn't answer. I couldn't look at her after being stripped of my essence the way I had.

I focused on one plank of the wooden floor, tracing the knots and the grain with my stare. Trying to process, or maybe trying not to process, what had just happened.

"Astrid, talk to me!" Lyric sounded frantic.

"I'm fine." I whispered the lie so that Lyric would stop worrying. "It's fine."

"You're sweating."

"It's hot in here."

"Astrid, you're never hot. What did he do to you?"

"I said it's fine." I looked up to meet her tear-filled eyes. I had to be stronger than I was. Taking a shuddering breath, I repeated, "I'm okay, Lyric. We're okay."

"What was that? What did he do to you?"

Whatever it was, I felt too ashamed to talk about it. "We'll find a way to get out of here. Just let me think, okay?"

She nodded. I let my head rest against the wall behind me as I closed my eyes. Sweat trickled down the back of my neck.

. . .

Over the next two days, they fed us three square meals a day, always some kind of bland version of oatmeal, and kept us on our chains like animals. The heat in the cell was grueling. It made the stench of being in close quarters with the guards even worse.

Every day, twice a day, the circle tattoo guy would come in for a visit. He always used slow, deliberate movements, and he always came in and touched my face. Each time, his touch was agonizing and stripped something away from my very core. It also never felt less violating.

I put on a brave face for my sister. But I didn't know how much longer I could endure the torture that left me exhausted, drenched in sweat, and feeling like a mere shell.

The guards rotated through, but they always came in sets of two and seemed to be universally fond of playing cards. Lyric and I had given them each insulting monikers. We looked for a pattern in the rotation. Hoping to find a weakness in their security. We hadn't found one.

I continually demanded answers as to why I was being tortured. There didn't seem to be anyone who spoke English, let alone who cared to tell me what they wanted from me. Maybe it was just a twisted form of entertainment. At least they weren't using Lyric for their sport. That would have been unbearable.

The third day started out the same, a visit from the tattooed creature who touched my face and made me feel like I was dying, followed by a meal and plenty of clean water.

I was grateful for the abundance of water to drink. Lyric wasn't bothered by the heat, whereas I was dying. Lyric and I thought maybe my body was in trauma from the torture and couldn't regulate. The other weird side effect was that, despite the fact that I didn't have my medication, I hadn't experienced even the whisper of a headache since I'd been shut in the cell with Lyric. A feat no medication had ever accomplished for three days in a row.

Halfway through the third day, a lone guard we didn't recognize came in. He wore a belt of weapons unlike the other guards. After a brief conversation with the two on-duty guards, the former pair left, and we were alone with the newcomer. He grabbed the keys off the table and approached the cell. Worried, I glanced at my sister, her face full of distress.

The goblin casually let himself into the cell with us and approached Lyric, speaking in the strange language.

"Leave her alone." I tried to fill my voice with defiance and menace, hoping it would be enough. I was still chained to the wall, and exhausted, there was nothing else I could do.

The goblin hardly spared me a glance before speaking to her in accented English. His voice was strange, like he was hitting two notes at the same time. "I will not hurt you. I am a friend. We can help each other."

"If you want to help us, then get us out of this place." She held up her shackled hands.

"I can only help you." He pointed at my sister's face. "Only room for one."

"Then help my sister." Lyric said, jerking her head slightly to indicate where I sat across the cell.

"No." I shook my head. "I won't leave without you, Lyric."

The goblin didn't even glance my way. "I can only help you."

Lyric jutted her chin out. "I won't leave without my sister."

"The Jalak Brotherhood will come after us if I take their power source." As though that explained everything. Or anything.

"What does that mean?" I demanded.

The goblin grumbled a bit and then turned to face me. "I can only help her. I'm sorry."

"How do I know you're going to *help*?" I leaned towards him. "What makes you different from the rest of your friends that kidnapped us?"

The goblin looked all around the room as though worried we were being watched. Then he turned to look between my sister and me. "I will show you, but you keep quiet."

Lyric and I looked at each other before she said, "We'll keep quiet."

"As long as you don't come near us," I added.

The goblin nodded and took a step back.

His form rippled, and suddenly his green skin became a beautiful dark brown. He was human, with a muscular frame and a pleasant face. He still had a bald head, but it was smooth. His eyes were brown and friendly—they crinkled when he smiled.

When he spoke, his voice was deep, and he had a thick Jamaican accent. "I am a shapeshifter."

What the...?

I must have worn my thoughts on my face because his smile turned into a laugh that rumbled through the air.

"Oh my word, that was so cool!" Lyric's eyes were wide,

and her hands had flown to her mouth. She moved them slightly to add, "Is this your real form?"

"It is." He gave a slight bow. "I am Roshaun Buhari. You can call me Ro. I am one of the last of the Toban race in the Realm of Light."

"The what?" My brain was shorting out. There was no logical explanation for what I had just seen. In fact, there was no logic to a lot of things I'd been seeing the last three days.

"I cannot risk keeping this form. If the Jalak Brotherhood discover that I hide among them, we will all be in danger."

"Why are you hiding here?" I asked.

"I came to help my rebel friends in the Realm of Light." He took a step towards Lyric when he spoke, nodding his head a bit. "When I leave in two days, I can take you with me."

She narrowed her silver eyes at him. "I told you, I'm not leaving Astrid."

Ro looked at me, "You are valuable to the Jalak because of your magic. They siphon it to recharge their talismans. If you go missing, they will hunt us down."

"Let me stop you right there." I held up my hands. "Did you say magic?"

"Yes. Your magic is unlike any I've ever felt. Though admittedly, I am not a skilled magic sensor."

"Okay, well, I don't have magic." I shook my head, unwilling to accept what he was saying. "Magic isn't real."

"Astrid, what if it is? You saw what he just did," Lyric said. She had always had a whimsical heart. It made sense for her to believe in magic after what we'd just seen.

"It's not." My tone came out flat. But even as I said it, my mind reeled at the possibilities.

I'd seen Ro change forms. I'd seen the goblins. I'd seen the ship and the green mist, and I remembered how strange it had made me feel. I'd also felt stripped bare every time the tattoo goblin touched my face.

What if magic is the explanation for all of it?

When I allowed myself to think the thought, it shifted everything in my world just a little.

What if magic explained the power that I could feel being ripped from me when the goblin touched me? Maybe I had never known it was there, but it felt familiar all the same.

But Lyric is the one we have spent our lives protecting. I'm nothing special.

"Magic has been extinct for thousands of years on Earth," Ro was explaining to Lyric, "but it thrives in the Realm of Light."

"What's the Realm of Light?" Lyric asked.

"It is the place where we are traveling to. Through portals, travel can happen between the Realm of Light, the Realm of Stars, and the Realm of Shadows. Though, the Realm of Shadows has gone dark since the magic stopped flowing through the Realm of Stars."

"The Realm of Stars?" I asked.

"It is the realm where you came from."

I shook my head to refocus, not wanting to be distracted from the original topic.

"Where will you take Lyric when you escape with her?"

"I'm not going anywhere without you, Astrid." Lyric spoke, but I ignored her.

"I will take her to the rebel base where my friends are."

"Why are you offering to help?" My tone skeptical of his intentions.

"I am here to steal trinkets to fund the rebellion." He waved his hand. "I'm not interested in being a part of kidnappings."

"How do I know we can trust you?"

"I have given you my true identity. I cannot give more than that. You will need to have faith."

"I'm pretty low on faith right now. You'll have to do better than that."

After a moment, he nodded and said, "I will unchain you so you can move inside the cell freely. I will bring you a change of clothes, and I will even have the soiled clothes you wear washed."

I nodded once. "That's a good start." Not because it would suddenly help me trust his intentions, but because I desperately wanted to get out of the urine-soaked clothes we wore, and to be unchained. Right now, we couldn't even reach the bucket.

"Astrid, I will *not* go without you." Lyric said again.

Ro turned to her. "I cannot take her without risking us all."

"Lyric, I will be fine. If you get out, that's half the battle."

She looked into Ro's face, her ethereal eyes flashing with a menace I rarely saw in her. "If you think you can take me without taking Astrid, I promise you, I will raise so much hell that you will get caught and never see anyone you love again. Do you hear me!?"

After a long silence, and the stare down of the century, Ro sighed. "I hear you. I cannot promise that it's possible, but I will try to think of something."

He unlocked our manacles before leaving the cell and locking the door behind him.

Finally able to move, my sister and I held tight to each other. "We're staying together, or we're going together," she whispered.

"Okay." I said. Though I knew that if there was a chance to save her, I would sacrifice myself to make it happen.

As promised, Ro came back with a simple pair of brown cotton pants and shirt for each of us, as well as a bucket of water and a bar of hard soap. We cleaned up and changed while he stood facing the door of the room to give us privacy. He had his goblin form on and while totally creepy, nothing could detract from the bliss of being semi-clean. A privilege I didn't think I would ever take for granted again.

After we'd washed and changed, we washed our dirty clothes, and I laid them in the corner to dry. Then I laid down and slept more peacefully than I had in days.

I awoke with the arrival of our dinner. The goblin who delivered it didn't give us a second look. Ro was sitting at the table in his goblin form. I could tell it was him because of the weapons belt he wore. The pattern of the day told me that my tormentor would soon visit. I asked Ro about the goblin with the circle tattoos around his eyes.

"Brother Miaal," he said. "He's one of the few Jalak who can siphon magic from other sources—as long as the source is pliable." He gave me a raised eyebrow look, and I got the feeling he was unimpressed with the fact that I allowed the siphoning to happen.

"Is there a way to resist him?"

"Well, if there wasn't," he gave me a meaningful look, "they would take magic from a lot more people."

"Can you show me?" I stepped forward, hope glimmering in my chest.

"Guard change comes soon." He shook his head. "There is not time for lessons."

"What do the goblins do with the magic they're taking from her?" Lyric asked.

"The Jalak store the magic they take from others in talismans. Some they keep on their persons to power the spells and craft that they can't otherwise do. Some they sell."

"Goblin thieves," I scoffed. "It's all so unbelievable."

"The Jalak Brotherhood are pirates of magic. They scavenge and pillage it from both of the realms."

"I thought you said there were three realms?" Lyric said.

"No one who travels to the Realm of Shadows ever returns."

"Great. How do we send their asses there?" I planted my hands on my hips. I would love nothing more than to banish them all to hell.

Ro didn't respond. He just looked at me with something like sympathy in his eyes.

"How do they pillage magic from Earth if magic is extinct there?" Lyric didn't sound skeptical, just curious.

"They don't often go to Earth, since Earth magic has run dry, There's not usually much to find." He gestured towards us. "They were lucky finding you."

Yes... so lucky.

"If people have magic in the Realm of Light, then who buys these talismans?" Lyric's questions, usually endearing, felt like a small betrayal. I didn't want to sit and chat about magic. In my mind, it was an irritating new reality that had ruined our lives.

"The different races can only do certain things with their magic. Sometimes it is worth buying an artifact or talisman that is filled with magic that differs from your own." Ro just kept answering Lyric's questions. "When it's not magic they're selling, it's slaves."

"Slaves?" Lyric looked horrified.

Ro shrugged. "They take non magical people from the Realm of Stars and sell them as slaves in the Realm of Light. The Fae are notably fond of this type of merchandise."

"Is that why they took me and Tyler?" Lyric suddenly looked as horrified as I felt. The silent sense of camaraderie I felt propelled my irritable mood into protective anger.

"I won't let them sell you, Lyric." I promised.

Ro shook his head. "You have the silver eyes. You are too valuable to ever be sold as a slave."

"But they'll sell Tyler as a slave?" Lyric looked at me. "Astrid, we have to get him out of here. He's in this mess because he was trying to help me."

"We have to get out of this cell before we can help Tyler. But we're going to try." I hoped the promise wasn't in vain.

Before we could continue the conversation, the door to the room opened. Ro turned towards the table, pretending to be absorbed in something there. Brother Miaal stepped into view.

Anger and dread flared in my chest when I saw the goblin

in his dark robe with his hands of terror. Right on schedule for my nightly torture session. I swallowed hard.

Ro had mentioned that it would be best if I cooperated, so that I didn't draw any suspicion from the Jalak about our budding escape plans. Especially in light of the fact that we were no longer in our chains. I didn't want to cooperate, but I didn't want to ruin our chance for escape.

Brother Miaal took one look at my sister and I, unchained and in new clothes. Then turned to Ro speaking in harsh snarling words. Ro explained something in the Jalak tongue, and then the two of them stepped into the cell. Ro whispered something to Lyric as he passed by her, and then took my arms and pinned my elbows back, holding me tight against his chest. He whispered in my ear. "Cooperate." My hands, though restrained, were poised to attack the goblin about to touch me.

I had little time to react because, as Ro held me to keep me from lashing out, Brother Miaal grabbed my face.

The siphoning began. Power flowed out of me. Now that I was aware of what was happening, it was so obvious that it was power being ripped away from me—that's exactly what it felt like. I clenched my teeth and closed my mind to the pain, channeling all of my rage into how much I wanted to ruin this goblin's life.

Consumed with pain, I pictured Brother Miaal engulfed in the flames of my hate for him. I put all of my focus into that image. When I couldn't hold back my screams any longer, they ripped through my clenched teeth.

With my scream came a surge of energy from deep in my core. It traveled up through my arms and out through my hands. The same moment the sound escaped my mouth, a burst of red light came from each of my palms and incinerated the goblin before me.

The creature didn't even burst into flames. He simply went from being there, touching my skin, to glowing bright red from within. Then he was smoke and ash lightly falling to the ground. The moment Brother Miaal was gone, the pain stopped. Ro removed his hands from my arms and stepped away from me. Without the strength to stand, I slumped to my knees. My entire body trembled.

A pile of ashes sat where a living person had been only moments before.

Did I do that?

I didn't ask the question aloud. I knew that I had. The power I'd wielded felt so foreign and yet so familiar. What kind of monster was I? An out-of-control moment and I'd ended a life without even trying.

FIVE

The rough wood of the cell floor beneath my hands and knees grounded me in reality.

"What was that?" Lyric sounded scared.

She's afraid of me. I don't blame her.

Somewhere in the peripheral of my mind, I recognized Ro and Lyric talking, but I couldn't focus on what they were saying. I felt so ashamed, I didn't want to look up at them.

Is this why Mom was so secretive?

Am I the reason Lyric needed protection?

I had wanted to ruin his life, and make him stop hurting me, but I hadn't meant to kill anyone.

Am I evil?

What kind of magic is this that I can kill without a word?

Killer... I couldn't make sense of my new identity.

How had I never known this power was there before?

Can I get rid of it?

So many questions and no one I could ask. I needed my mother.

Did she know about this magic? If she did, why didn't she tell me?

My goal in life, for as long as I could remember, was protecting Lyric. My life was a lie. It turned out Lyric most needed protection from me.

Magic is a fairytale for children. This is a nightmare.

I was afraid that I would lose my cool and accidentally hurt my sister—one of the only people I really cared about.

I would die if I hurt her.

I couldn't say how long I sat in my cocoon of harrowing thoughts, but a soft touch on my shoulder pulled me out. My body tensed. Afraid of what could happen if I even moved.

"Astrid?" The hesitation in Lyric's whisper told me she was afraid, too. I wondered how she'd even found the courage to touch me.

Then her slender arms wrapped around me.

"It was an accident," She said, laying her head on top of mine.

The gesture cracked me open. My body gave way to silent, racking sobs. My shaking arms responded, and I held onto Lyric; because in that moment, my soul had no other anchor.

Ro left us alone like that, crying in each other's arms. It didn't take long for Jalak to swarm the room in a panic, and, too soon, my sister and I were ripped apart. They left Lyric alone, but chained me up again. I had no strength to stand, let alone fight. I'd never truly experienced fatigue until this. Apparently, using magic drained me more than the siphoning sessions.

. . .

According to Lyric, I was dead to the world for a full two days. Since Ro only did guard duty periodically, my sister was impatient to have someone to talk to. Now that I was awake, she rattled on about several things without my having to contribute much to the conversation.

"The ship changed course," Lyric said. "I guess the Jalak Brotherhood wanted to go to their lands and pick up another guy with siphon powers."

I groaned in response. I didn't even want to think about another goblin with siphoning power. I finally sat up. Physically I felt alright. I wasn't about to run a marathon or anything. I was still near empty in my core, but I was rested and still migraine free.

"Ro and I had to improvise plans without you." Her tone was all business now. "Ro says it's best if we escape when we dock tonight instead of waiting to be near the capital."

"The capital?"

"That's where we were headed before." Lyric nodded. "I guess it's close to Fae lands where the Jalak Brotherhood plan to sell their slaves." Lyric hesitated for a moment before adding, "And where they're taking me."

The thought of having Lyric close to being sold or trafficked had my brain instantly on alert.

"I agree we should get off here." I stood. I gathered my clothes from where they were clean and dry in the corner.

"The only problem is that this stop is also a bit of a way from the rebel base," she said.

"So?" Not caring that there were guards in the room, I began changing into my own comfortable clothes.

"So that's where we have to go to get his friends to help us."

The fact that we were not even on Earth was hard to take in.

I took a moment to think and then voiced my idea. "Maybe we can just lie low and hop on the next ship back to Earth."

"I suggested that." Lyric began changing into her own clothes as well. "But Ro says not many people realm travel. Plus, it takes a ship that is outfitted with some kind of special travel stones. Which, I guess, are hard to find."

The implication of what she was saying was that we'd be here for a while. "Which gives the goblins lots of time to find us with their magic sensing abilities."

"They're Jalak," she said. "But yes."

I considered suggesting that we separate, so she wouldn't be endangered by my magic, or by the Jalak sensing my magic. But separating terrified me almost as much as my magic did.

"So the only problem is..." She wrung her hands together.

"What?" I braced myself for her to tell me she was leaving me behind.

"Well," she hedged. "Ro won't agree to bring Tyler. He says just you and me."

"There's a shocker."

"But we can't leave him!" Lyric grabbed my arm, her face full of pleading.

What did she expect us to do? We were going to be lucky to get out at all. Everything we did was going to flare up her chronic fatigue syndrome and exhaust her, as it was. Adding a pitstop would seriously hinder her chances at getting home.

I took a heavy breath. "As much as I care about Tyler, I'm not risking your safety to help him."

"Well, I have an idea that would work for everyone."

"Which is?"

"If you break Tyler out and meet back up with us after we're all off the ship—"

"No way." I held up a hand. "We're not splitting up."

I'm not trusting Ro with your safety.

"Just hear me out!"

I raised my eyebrows. I wouldn't agree to what she wanted, but I could at least let her feel heard. I gestured for her to continue.

She went on in a rush. "We've already mapped out a meeting place. It's perfect! No one will find us, and Ro says that splitting up might be even less dangerous for me because it gives the Jalak something else to focus on."

Lyric threw that last part in because she knew it was the lynchpin of her argument. She knew I would put her safety first, every time.

"If you agree to get Tyler out and meet up with us, I'll never ask you for anything else in my life, Astrid. I swear!"

There was no way that would hold true, but it didn't matter. My priority was her safety. I just didn't know if I could trust Ro, and it scared me to let Lyric out of my sight.

"Astrid, I'm begging you." Tears welled in her eyes. She could see me calculating the risks, and she didn't like it.

"You promised we would help him." Her chin quivered.

I hated it. There was enormous risk either way. But if I

could give Lyric her best chance and also help Tyler, she was right. It was clearly the best option.

Plus, I cared about Tyler. If Lyric hadn't been part of the equation, I wouldn't have even considered leaving him behind.

"If anything happens to you while we're separated, I swear..."

She threw her arms around my neck. "Thank you!"

Lyric began outlining the details of the plan that they had come up with while I'd been recovering. Ro had drawn a two-sided map for me. One side would take me to the cell where the slaves were kept. He never did guard duty down there, so he could only get me to the room, not the right cage. The other side of the map was drawn from the docks to the rendezvous point where we would meet up with Lyric, and I would never again let her out of my sight. I even thought about bringing her to classes with me when we got home.

We have to get home first, Astrid... We're a long way from Kansas City.

When the Jalak brought our dinner—more bland oatmeal crap—I ate ferociously. A lot of my strength came back after sleep, but eating was key. I still felt drained in a deep-down way.

"What was it like?" Lyric asked as she picked at her oatmeal. "Using the magic, I mean."

Not ready to talk about it, I shoved the last bite of oatmeal in my mouth before shrugging and gesturing to her bowl. "Are you gonna eat that?"

She traded her mostly untouched bowl for my empty one. "I imagine it gave you a headache, huh?" A safe assumption, since most strenuous things usually gave me a headache.

"No, I still haven't had a headache since I got here," I said.

"So, did it hurt when the fire came out of your hands?"

I shook my head no and tried to push the rising shame back down, so that I could keep eating.

"How did you know what to do to use your power?" Her tone was full of curiosity.

I set the spoon down in the mostly empty bowl and pushed the tray away. "I didn't," I said without taking my eyes off of the spoon.

"Well how did you do it?" I could tell she was trying to be patient and give me space, but was tired of being put off.

I finally met her gaze. "I was just angry and wanted to make him stop hurting me." Admitting that I lost control because of my anger felt humiliating, so I rushed past it. "The red light came out of nowhere."

"So, it could happen again at any moment?" She folded her arms and gave me a look that said she wasn't buying it.

"No! Of course not." I mimicked the gesture. "I don't know how I did it, okay? I wish I did. I was thinking about how I hated him and wanted to hurt him back, and suddenly... he was gone."

There. I'd said the awful truth. I'd wanted to hurt him.
I am evil.

Lyric stepped over and put her hands on my shoulders, forcing me to look into her face. "You acted in self-defense. No one can fault you for that."

"I'm pretty sure there's an entire ship full of goblins who fault me for it."

"Well, they kidnapped us. So let's agree that their moral opinions don't count."

I laughed. "You're totally right."

"I'm glad we're here together at least." Lyric swayed a bit and used the wall to steady herself as she sat down.

"Are you okay?" I reached out a hand to her.

"I'm fine." She waved me off. "It's just a chair day."

"Well, I guess you should have had the kidnappers bring your wheelchair along." I rolled my eyes in her direction.

"Yeah, what was I thinking?" She smiled, and we laughed.

Long after the Jalak took away the dinner dishes the shapeshifter came into the room relieving the other guards. Once they were gone, his form shimmered, and human Ro appeared. He dug into his deep pockets and handed something to Lyric through the bars.

"Thank you!" She held up her phone for me to see. "It's dead, but at least I'll have it when we get home!"

He handed me my phone along with my beloved wrist cuff.

"Oh my gosh!" I snatched it and hugged it to my chest, suddenly flooded with emotion. "I thought I lost it forever."

Relief at having it back washed through me. I rubbed the familiar amber stone and secured it to my arm in its rightful spot.

Ro smiled warmly, then handed my sister and me each a gnarly looking Jalak dagger. I really hoped I wouldn't need to use it—having to stab someone seemed even worse than accidental magic-fire murder. I didn't want to be a killer, but I wasn't going to be stupid and refuse to protect myself. I reminded myself that these goblins kidnapped us and I would have to be ready to do what needed to be done. I secured the leather sheath around my thigh.

Ro held up his two-sided map. "The crew is getting ready to bed down. It's almost time. Let's go over the routes."

I shivered and looked around for the source of the new chill in the air. The door wasn't open. Maybe the port was an arctic part of this realm.

I turned back to Ro who was explaining the map he'd drawn to where Tyler was being held. I started getting an aura and dizziness and had to focus all my concentration on the map in front of me. The strain of my eyes created a throbbing in my head.

Ugh, this is the worst possible time to finally have a migraine!

Lyric looked at me questioningly. "Are you okay?"

"I'm getting a stress headache." I squeezed my eyes tight, then opened them, hoping that the aura would be gone. It wasn't.

"You can do this." My sister gave my hand a reassuring squeeze. I nodded and smiled to reassure her.

After Ro had walked me through his maps and we'd recapped the plan again, I insisted on directions to the rebel base, in case we missed each other at the rendezvous point. I didn't want to take any chances. Ro had begrudgingly explained how to get there–directions that were supposed to be highly secret. I worked to commit them to memory, since they weren't mapped out. Finally, it was time to go.

My hands were cold and clammy, and I shivered from

chill and anxiety. My mind started going over all the things that might go wrong, letting this man in goblin form take my sister somewhere without me.

Stop it, Astrid. For once in your life, you need to trust and let someone help you.

I gave Lyric an extra tight hug and a quick kiss on the cheek. Her beautiful face looked pale. She was clearly weak, and it killed me to be letting her out of my sight.

I turned to Ro. "She really should be in her wheelchair. You might need to carry her sometimes. Just please, be careful."

"Don't worry about me, Astrid," Lyric said. "I'll manage."

We parted ways. I glanced back several times to see Ro helping Lyric along until I couldn't see them anymore.

At last I pulled open the map. The pain in my head blurred my vision, and I massaged my temple as I stooped in the shadows, working hard to memorize the directions on the first side of the map.

It ended up being fairly easy to get to the slave quarters of the ship following Ro's instructions, especially because most of the Jalak were already asleep.

Once I got to the slave room, I used the key Ro had given me to unlock the door. It swung on its hinges with a creaking sound, which to me seemed like a blaring trumpet announcing my arrival. I froze in place, my entire body convulsing with shivers. The stench of sewage and puke wafting from the now-open doorway made my stomach turn. Was the air fit to breathe? Raising one arm to cover my face with the sleeve of my crop top, I glanced around. No one had come running to investigate the creaking noise. I was grateful that the boat creaked and groaned all the time. Fighting pain and nausea, I crept into the dimly lit room. Two Jalak guards lay asleep at a table with empty glasses—their drinks a gift from Ro.

Relief filled me.

You've proven reliable this far, buddy. You'd just better keep my sister safe.

The prisoners sat in cages that resembled dog crates, lining the walls and stacked three high. The figures inside were mostly sleeping as well, but a few weren't—their wide eyes watched me. I put my finger to my mouth to show that they should be silent. I didn't want to rely too heavily on Ro's sleeping drugs. I accidentally breathed in while my sleeve was away from my nose and almost puked up my dinner.

I thought of the knife strapped to my thigh.

Should I kill the Jalak in order to keep them from waking? No.

This wasn't a spy movie.

While I had killed before, it had been an accident.

I swallowed down my disgust at the memory and tip-toed over to the cages, looking into each one.

As silently as I could manage, I took the keys off of the hook near the guard table and made my way down the aisles of crates.

Every prisoner had a metal collar around their neck. My heart broke for these people, some who were old, some who I guessed were as young as fifteen. I inspected every face, looking for Tyler.

At the end of the row lay a little girl, curled up in the corner of her crate, the light from the porthole illuminating the stains of dried tears on her dirty cheeks. The way her bottom lip was sucked into her mouth as she slept reminded me of Lyric as a child. An angry stillness came over me as my blood did an 'aw, hell no' in my veins. She looked to be about six or seven.

A sneer of hate twisted my face at the thought of the goblins who had taken this child from her family and chained her up like a dog.

My decision was made—I wouldn't leave a single prisoner here in this place. It would only help to distract from Lyric's escape if I got caught here helping these people. Searching down the second row of crates, I found Tyler. His tall legs were crammed up against his chest, and he slept with this cheek pressed to the metal of the cage. I used the keys to unlock the door as quietly as I could. Two prisoners who were awake lurched forward, whispering something I couldn't make out. I again raised my finger to my lips, desperate for them to be quiet.

I reached into Tyler's open cage and gently touched his knee. He flinched away from me, his green eyes full of terrors. His matted red hair hit the top of the crate, and filth covered his freckled face. Red-hot anger burned in my core. *How can anyone treat people this way.*

When he recognized me, his face relaxed in relief. "Astrid!?"

"Shhh." I helped him out of the cage.

He winced as he stretched one leg and then the other.

He hissed in pain as he stood to his full height for the first time in probably days. "Did you find Lyric?"

"Yeah, I found her," I said, then put a hand on his arm. "Hey, while I'm rescuing you, and you're happy to see me, I wanted to tell you—I stole your bike. I'm sorry... but the door of my apartment was broken, and Lyric was missing and—"

"Astrid." He limped a bit and put an arm around my shoulders. "I'm pretty sure that poor timing is supposed to be my thing, not yours." He shook his leg a bit. "And I can't believe I'm saying this, but we have more important things to worry about right now than my bike."

"Right." I nodded up at him. "You're right. We need to get everyone out of these cages." I gestured to his leg. "Can you walk?"

"Yeah, no problem... my foot's just asleep."

I turned to go.

"But hey," he caught my arm. "Is she okay?"

"Lyric or your bike?"

He shrugged. "Both."

I rolled my eyes.

"I'm kidding!" he whispered. "You know humor is my coping mechanism. Of course I was talking about Lyric."

"She's good. We're going to meet up with her. Come on."

"Can you get this collar off of me? It's locked with some kind of key I've never seen before, but they keep all the keys over on the—"

Before he could finish, I had his collar off, courtesy of the ring of Jalak keys. Then I gave him the key to the cage doors, and we went assembly line style down the cages, freeing prisoners.

Several of them made a little too much noise for my

liking, and a few of them straight up made a lot of noise—the ingrates. The sleeping guards in the room didn't wake, but the door to the room was rattling with someone trying to come in. Apparently we'd garnered some attention from other guards.

Tyler and I freed most of the prisoners and turned to face the new guards who had just burst through the door. Upon seeing our handiwork, they began screaming in their animalistic tongue, weapons at the ready, trying to herd the prisoners back to their cages.

We were cornered. We were all going to die.

I thought of how I'd used my magic to kill Brother Miaal.

I thought about the little girl in the cage, and all the other people here fighting to survive. To be free.

These goblins are monsters.

I wouldn't allow myself to feel bad for hurting them to save people.

"Stand back!" I yelled.

Hopefully the prisoners could understand me. And would trust me.

I desperately tried to summon the red flame from my gut. All I got was a massive spike to my headache that about knocked me over.

"Crap!" I looked up at Tyler. "What do we do?"

"Panic?"

"Not helpful." I looked around desperately for some way to escape.

"You know what they say. Panicking burns a shit ton of calories."

"Who says that?" I grabbed my knife.

"I said it, just now."

The guards were busy for the moment, rounding up the prisoners closest to them. We were trapped in the back of the room, the only way out blocked.

"Cover me." I handed Tyler my knife and turned to face the wall behind us.

I closed my eyes and tried to calm my mind through the blinding pain. I took three breaths deep into my belly and searched for the power that I'd felt when the Jalak priest siphoned from me that last time. Surrendering to that moment, I remembered the pain. I felt the rage. I searched for my power.

Finally, I latched onto it—a distant whisper of the power I'd felt before, but that made sense. I was probably still drained from last time.

"Umm, Astrid..." Tyler said.

"Shhh." I mentally caressed the power and tried to coax it into rallying.

"What are you doing back there, Astrid?!"

"I'm trying to concentrate." I pressed my eyes closed harder.

"You might want to do it faster."

"Not helpful."

"More guards just showed up."

The fear in my chest caused me to lose my mental grip on the power. I huffed in frustration.

"We're gonna die." Tyler's tone was getting higher.

"Tyler, just watch my back. I need a minute."

"Okay, but I'm counting. One..."

"Tyler!" I snapped.

"Right, sorry. In my head."

I took several calming breaths. This time, when I found

the tiny flicker of power deep in my core, I didn't bother trying to coax or caress, I just flung it up through me.

A small orb of red light bloomed between my palms. I turned and hurled it at the guards that were closing in on us.

It did not hit the target.

Instead, it took out a chunk of wall in a fiery explosion.

Most of the guards ran scared, clearly unaware of the fact that I'd just used all the magic I knew, and probably couldn't duplicate the stunt to save my life. The remaining two looked like they were about to follow their friends.

"Dude!" Tyler's face was filled with excitement. "A magical fireball? How did you do that? Can you teach me?"

"Not the time." I grabbed his arm and pulled him towards the last few cages that we still needed to open. All the prisoners were frantic. Some were jumping out of the ship via my newly installed flaming picture window. I reached the cage that held the little girl. We freed her, and I scooped her up. She recoiled away from me, and I tried to calm her. "I'm not going to hurt you. I'm here to help."

"Gemma!" A small, blond woman with a heart-shaped face, pushed her way through the crowd and grabbed the little girl from my arms.

"Mommy!" The girl clung to her.

"C'mon!" I urged the mother and daughter towards the opening. "Can you swim?"

"Barely. But Gemma can't, and there's no way I can swim for two," the mom said. "Is there another way?"

I looked back at the door where guards were amassing once again. "Nope." I looked at Tyler. "We're going to have to help her once we jump into the water."

"Okay, we'll tag team it." He bounced on his feet a little

as if hyping himself up. "I'm a better swimmer than you are, so I'll take Gemma first."

"Says who?"

"I was on the swim team for two years, and Lyric says you avoid swimming at all costs."

I rolled my eyes. My sister was a sellout.

Jalak were pouring into the room. It was now or never.

I tore Gemma from her mother, practically throwing the little girl into Tyler's arms. "Jump!"

He dove out with her.

Gemma's mother followed.

I stepped up to the fiery opening. Three moons hung in the sky, illuminating the night. There was an embankment not far away. We would have to swim and then climb. The cliff cast a dark shadow on the water. The entire scene was so vast, and the water so far below. I was frozen with terror. This is why I was afraid of heights. I couldn't bring myself to jump. Green hands grabbed at me, and I flung myself away to escape them.

My stomach met my throat as I fell. My lurching gut made screaming impossible. I hit the dark water feet first, and the chill on my skin caused instant goosebumps. The moment I went underwater, I started pumping my limbs to carry me to the surface. When I broke into the air, I gasped and whirled around, looking for Tyler. It was hard to spot him in the crowd, but I finally saw him—a tiny child clinging to his neck.

We didn't die. We're okay.

I took a moment to breathe. The opening of the ship high above us was ablaze and spreading fast. I smiled, knowing that my actions were causing the horrid ship to burn.

I was glad Tyler had taken the girl. Using my magic again had drained what little I'd replenished. I was weary. Once my body was used to the cool water, I realized it wasn't freezing. Pumping my arms and legs kept me at a comfortable temperature. The longer we paddled, the more the water almost felt rejuvenating. I had swimming skills for mere survival, so between me and Gemma, making our way to shore was slow. Land seemed much further away than it had from up in the ship.

Yard by yard, we made our way to shore.

I wished that we had been able to get a lifeboat like the original plan entailed. Thinking of how Lyric and Ro had made this journey by rowboat only a short time before, I was a little jealous.

Tyler was a trooper, keeping himself and Gemma afloat, but he needed a break, and I couldn't do what he was doing. Gemma's mother found a piece of wood from the ship. Though charred and only big enough to fit under the girl's small arms, it allowed her to float. Tyler and her mother, on each side, helped to guide her along as she whimpered and barely kicked her legs.

The brief peace I was feeling was shattered when the Jalak Brotherhood started lowering boats into the water.

Crap.

"We have to move faster!" I said.

Our little group swam harder. Would it be enough?

Six

J alak in their boats were collecting their scattered prisoners right and left. My heart ached for the people being recaptured. The shadow from the reef made it hard to see, and if the goblins were looking for me specifically, the darkness was my saving grace.

We reached the jagged reef as two boats were closing in on our location. We dragged our bodies from the water and scrambled up the face of the steep incline. The rocks scraped my hands. I ignored the pain. Touching the earth even in this strange place somehow recharged me after being at sea for so many awful days.

Jalak swarmed all around. Several were climbing up behind us.

"Faster!" I shouted.

When we finally got to level ground where the footing became softer, we stumbled forward. There was no time to take in the strange realm. Tyler and I ran with the girl and her mother between us. The ground was sandy but not nice sand, like the beach I'd once visited in Florida. This terrain was rough and full of weeds and dotted with bushes. We no longer had the protection of the shadow from the bluff. The three moons gave a lot more light than the one on Earth. The light helped me keep track of Tyler. The prisoners the Jalak hadn't caught scrambled onto shore here and there. The threat of recapture kept us all moving.

The Jalak shouted behind us, their feet thundering in the sand. We ran harder. My eyes scanned for a place to hide.

To the left, a village lay nestled down the hill. I knew the rendezvous point was down there somewhere. We couldn't go that way. Lyric and Ro were waiting to meet up with us, but with the Jalak closing in, I wasn't going to lead them anywhere near Lyric.

To the right stood a lighthouse far in the distance.

Straight ahead lay a forest. I pointed—a wordless command. Tyler nodded. We ran for the trees. I hoped the forest would be dense enough to lose our pursuers once inside. The little girl and her mother followed. I didn't look back to see how close the Jalak were. With many of the prisoners recaptured, there were only a few groups left to pursue. Blessedly, we'd mostly gone in different directions, so the Jalak would have to split up to chase us.

We ran at a frantic pace. Gemma's mother tripped, her small frame hitting the ground hard. She began screaming. Tyler and I tried to pull her up and discovered she'd landed on a small thorny bush. I pulled out a branch of long purple and white thorns from her neck, face, and chest, as she screamed.

Horrified, I looked at Tyler. His expression mirrored my own thoughts.

This is bad. This is so bad.

The puncture wounds went deep. She staggered up, and we made our way forward, but she couldn't move very fast. Tyler and I helped her along, though it was agony to go at such a pace.

We're all going to get captured again.

Yards away from the cover of the trees, she dropped to her knees. "Gemma, baby." She was gasping. "No matter what happens, I love you. Do you hear me?" She held her daughter in a tearful embrace.

By the light of the moons, I could see dark spidery lines spreading out from her wounds. Some kind of infection or poison? She pushed away from her daughter and vomited. Tyler and I tried to pull her up, but she collapsed completely, unable to even sit.

The Jalak were getting close.

"We have to go!" I urged her to get up.

Her breathing became ragged. The wounds on her neck seemed to decay before our eyes. Sweat dripped down her temples, and she lay on the ground, writhing in agony.

"We have to go!" Tyler pulled at my arm. I understood what he meant. We had to leave her behind.

"No!" It was so horrible. I looked at Gemma, who was clearly terrified. I wouldn't let her lose her mother like I'd lost mine.

The woman grabbed my arm and looked into my face, foamy drool beginning to drip from her mouth. Through gritted teeth, she said, "Gemma."

"She's here," I said.

"Take... her... home." She gasped for air.

I nodded. "I will." A lump constricted my throat.

The woman grabbed my wet shirt and pulled me closer. "Swear it!"

"I promise you." I nodded. "I swear it."

The woman's grip loosened, and I sat back. My chest heaved with shallow breaths.

Gemma fell onto her mother's abdomen, begging her to get up, but her mother was already dead. My trembling fingers covered my gaping mouth.

The Jalak's vicious shouting spurred me into action. I dragged Gemma from her mother's corpse and ran with her sobbing and screaming in my ear. My head throbbed.

The girl was small, but I was already so tired.

The Jalak were gaining on us.

Tyler urged me to put her down so we could all run. We each grabbed one of her hands and pulled her along while her little legs pumped hard to keep up.

Cold wind assaulted our faces and my teeth chattered. Our wet clothes felt like weights. We reached the tree line with four Jalak close behind.

Once the darkness of the forest cloaked us, we veered to the right. I stumbled on a rock and almost fell. My heart clenched, afraid of finding another heinous thorny bush. I scrambled to keep pace. We swerved between trees and dodged branches.

Several small, hard objects struck me in the back.

Are they throwing rocks at us?

Without warning, Tyler hit the ground face first. The girl between us lurched suddenly towards me without the counter pull from Tyler.

"Tyler!" Looking back, I saw Tyler's prone body on the ground. Still as death. "No. No, no, no!"

"Hide!" I shoved the little girl down behind a fallen tree and turned to protect my friend.

I tried to summon the magic from my gut, but it wasn't there. I looked around, frantic. Grabbing a large rock, I hurled it toward the nearest Jalak. It hit the mark, but it didn't even slow him. Blindly, I hurled more rocks and sticks as I made my way to where Tyler's body lay. Tyler didn't stir or respond when I grabbed his arm. A small dart protruded from his neck. "Oh, my god, no!"

With trembling fingers, I plucked the dart out of Tyler's neck.

Picking up a good-sized branch, I wielded it like a baseball bat. Then I took a fighting stance over Tyler's still form to protect my two helpless companions.

The Jalak drew near. My body shook. I breathed a quiet prayer to whatever higher power in this universe might help me.

The nearest Jalak snarled and lunged, his yellow eyes glowing in the dark forest. The stench of his breath reached my face just as a terrifying whoosh sounded in my peripheral. A black blur flew in and snatched the goblin that had been just inches away from me. The remaining three goblins stopped and looked to the trees where their companion screamed.

The Jalak's cries cut off. His three companions shuffled side to side and looked frantically around. Another whoosh of air. The same black blur. A second Jalak gone. When the second goblin's screams abruptly cut off, the other two Jalak turned and ran. They only got a few steps before a third was picked off by the same black shadow.

Are we next?

My hands trembled as I crouched down to check for Tyler's pulse. He was still alive. Relief washed over me. As I looked up, the final goblin disappeared into the shadows.

The air whooshed again. I shielded my head, knowing what was coming.

Nothing happened.

Heart beating in my ears, I peeked from around my arms. There was the silhouette of a man with huge, dark wings.

Somewhere in my mind, I registered that I might be going into shock. I was looking into the shadowed face of what I could only assume was the god of death, and all I could do was stand there. Terrified. Gaping. Not an appropriate response.

Is he helping us? Or is he toying with me before he makes his kill?

He'd been just a blurred shadow before. He could catch me if I tried to run. I also couldn't leave Tyler and the little girl.

Shadows seemed to follow the figure as he stepped towards where I crouched defensively over Tyler's body.

The god of death spoke to me in a strange language, his deep voice reverberating in my body.

"I... can't understand you." My words came out in a breathy whisper. It surprised me that my voice worked at all, through the fear that gripped me.

His head tilted slightly, then he spoke again. "It's not a lethal poison."

"Huh?" Hearing his rumbling voice speak in English took a moment to process.

"The dart." The god of death gestured towards Tyler. "It knocked him out, but it won't kill him."

"How do you know that?"

"I can smell it."

"Oh."

"Besides, the Jalak like to keep their merchandise alive and valuable."

A whimper came from where the little girl hid. The shadow being and I both whipped our heads around towards the source. I stood slowly, trying not to make sudden movements so that Death wouldn't perceive me as a threat. My eyes darted back and forth between him and where I knew the little girl crouched.

"Please," I said, holding my hands up in a placating gesture. "Please leave her alone."

Death turned his dark face to look at me and then back towards the place where the girl peeked her little blond head up from behind a log.

"Is she yours?" He would have been scary in the dark woods, even if I hadn't just witnessed him easily kill four crazed goblins in the span of a mere minute.

"Yes... I mean... she's not actually mine, but I'm trying to keep her safe."

"And the weak male. He is yours too?"

"He's my friend." I kept my eyes on the dark-winged man. "Please don't hurt them."

. . .

Death made a rumbling sound in his throat and stepped closer to me, which brought his face halfway out of the shadows.

My breath caught. The god of death was a gorgeous specimen, with dark hair falling to his shoulders, and chiseled masculine features. Had I run into him on earth, as a regular man, I might have embarrassed myself trying to talk to him, and definitely would have made a point to fantasize about him later. But he was the same creature who had killed the goblins. He could kill me. I had to keep my attraction in check.

The god of death seemed to examine my soul with his piercing gray eyes. One of which were interrupted on the right side by a scar that ran to the middle of his cheek. The scar did nothing to diminish his sexiness.

His bat-like wings were gone—hidden away somewhere behind his muscular frame, as though I'd only imagined them. His clothes were dark, and in addition to a belt of weapons at his waist, a single leather strap ran diagonally across his chest.

Without opening his mouth, the man made another rumbling sound. His eyes tightened slightly.

Is he growling at me?

I didn't move, or even hardly breathe. Maybe he was deciding if I would be next on his hit list.

"What about you?" He said finally.

"Me?"

"You ask me not to hurt your friends."

I took a shaky breath. "Oh, I would very much like it if you also don't hurt me."

Another rumble. "Why are you here?"

"Well," I looked around at the dimly lit forest and back to where Death, half in shadow, stared me down with his beautiful, dangerous eyes. "I'm obviously not here to meet the locals."

He cocked an eyebrow.

Okay, he didn't appreciate my attempt at humor. "I was running for my life because the Jalak were after us, and this forest seemed a lot more promising than going back to the cells they had us in."

"You escaped the Jalak slavers?"

"Yes."

His face hardened as he turned his gaze to the forest rather than on me. He wore dark clothes with a leather jacket. After a few beats, he spoke again. "It isn't safe to be in these woods overnight. Follow me."

Since he was the most dangerous thing I'd seen in the forest so far, I didn't think it was a good idea to follow him back to his lair or whatever. Plus, I had to meet up with Lyric.

I was about to tell him 'no thank you', when he stepped forward and scooped Tyler up, tossing him over his broad shoulder.

"Wait, stop! Where are you taking him?"

Death didn't respond. He just started walking. I began to jog after him.

Wait, Gemma!

I darted back and grabbed her hand, pulling her along.

She whimpered and resisted. Clearly I wasn't the only one who was afraid to follow the god of death into the forest.

I bent down and scooped her up. "I'm going to protect you, okay? But we can't lose Tyler."

She bit her lip and buried her face in my neck.

I trudged forward.

"Wait!" I called after him. "I have to get to my sister."

He paused and turned. "Do the Jalak have her?"

"Not anymore. I'm supposed to meet her at..." I checked my wet pockets for the map and came up with nothing.

"Damn it!" I'd lost Ro's map somewhere between the ship and the forest.

How am I going to find Lyric?

"Where?"

"I don't know, but I have to find her." I set my jaw.

"Even with your magic hidden, the Jalak will find you before you find your sister." He turned and kept walking.

I hurried to keep up. "How do you know?"

"Because your scent is strong."

I ducked my head and tried to discreetly smell myself. It wasn't my fault I hadn't been able to shower in a while.

"Your friend will not wake from the poison for hours at least." His tone was indifferent. "With the storm coming in, you'll either follow me or go back to the slavers."

"I'm not going to let a little rain stop me from getting to my sister," I said under my breath.

"A storm is not a little rain in this land."

That sounds ominous.

Hold up. He could hear me?

If Tyler was out for very long, I couldn't wait here with him on the forest floor. I decided to stop worrying about it and let Death carry him to a safe place, then I would go find Lyric. We'd come back together for Tyler.

I held tight to Gemma, and followed Death as he made his way silently through the trees.

"So, what should I call you?" I asked. Better to ask than to call him "Death" to his face.

"My name is Kai."

Way less intense than the name I'd been using. "So, you're not the god of death?"

"No."

"Well, thanks for helping us, Kai." My headache spiked, and I swayed a bit while Gemma clung to my neck.

Belatedly I added, "I'm Astrid."

Kai just made that rumbling sound and kept walking.

Ugh, how did I get here? Following a weird guy deeper into the forest in the middle of the night?

We probably walked for a mile or two, but I couldn't be sure. I hoped he wasn't taking us back to his lair to torture and kill us slowly. My brain ran wild with all the scary movies I'd seen about vampires, demons, and mythical creatures.

Since he had Tyler, I followed and just prayed we'd all be okay. I might not have been using my best judgment, but who can tell when you're in a situation like that?

Now and then, the moonlight shone through the canopy enough that I could see that this place mostly resembled what you would see on Earth, except the colors here seemed more vivid, almost more alive. Some plants I recognized, but some had leaves that were large and foreign—kind of tropical looking. The trees had a slight purple hue to their white and brown bark. Combined with my migraine, it all made me feel like I was stuck in a very real, very bad dream.

The wind whipped through the trees more and more fiercely. I shivered. Maybe the storm was the reason my head hurt so much. I realized the storm that was kicking up was probably the kind that sent you to the basement back home. I half-expected to hear tornado sirens. My heart sank. There was no way I would find Lyric until the storm passed. I only hoped she and Ro had gotten to a safe shelter.

Finally, as rain began pelting our faces, Kai approached a generic-looking crop of foliage. He moved some vines to reveal an archway. We stepped through onto a path through the underbrush that wound around and finally opened up to a clearing. Lightning flashed in the sky and illuminated a small stone cottage nestled in halfway up the hillside. It was eerie. We hurried through the rain towards the house. Another long flash of lightning revealed a barn with a water wheel. It felt like stepping into an old western.

I hope it doesn't turn out to be a western horror.

We entered the cottage, which smelled of teak and lemon. There was nothing horror-esque in sight—as long as you didn't count the man that could sprout terrifying black wings, who brought us here. The large room, lit by two small lamps, had an array of quaint furniture, mostly made of wood. Embers glowed in the open fireplace. I smiled. I was getting Amish vibes, and this badass shadow man, Kai, did not fit the picture.

The piece that drew my eye was a large wood dining table with a natural edge. The grain of the wood was more dynamic than any I'd ever seen on Earth. Just like the trees in the forest, there was a subtle purple hue to it.

Despite everything, this home felt cozy. I breathed deeply and felt my shoulders relax a bit. My head was still throbbing, but the warmth of the fire was soothing.

Kai flopped Tyler down unceremoniously on the floor near the hearth.

"Don't throw him around!" I said, rushing over to make sure Tyler's head was okay, setting Gemma down next to me.

A door on the far side of the room thumped open. I whirled around. A woman with gray hair pulled over one shoulder in a long, thick braid rushed in. Seeing that she had a weapon in hand, I pushed Gemma behind me. The woman's skin looked worn in the lamplight, but her eyes were fierce, as she looked us over with a frown.

Her accent was almost Scottish. "Kai, what are you bringing into my home in the middle of the night?"

"They were being attacked." Kai began unstrapping his weapons from his body. The light of the fire flickered over his large biceps in a distracting way.

"We cannot take in strays!" The woman waved her hands wildly at us. "Out!"

"By Jalak slavers." Kai tilted his head in emphasis, as though it explained everything.

The woman raised an arched eyebrow. After a beat, she shrugged as though she understood but didn't like it.

I watched their exchange with curiosity.

What was that about?

She huffed. "Put them in your room then." She walked back into the room she came from.

That low rumbling sound came from Kai's throat again. Did the growl mean he was irritated then?

He took a lamp from the table and went into another adjacent room.

Gemma and I peeked around the corner where Kai had disappeared. It was a room with a simple bed, some clothes in piles, and weapons strewn all around.

I smirked. "Turns out he's a softy who lives with his mom." I'd said it so quietly it was almost like I didn't say it. Suddenly, he didn't seem at all scary anymore.

Apparently Kai really did have super-hearing, because he answered in a gruff tone. "This is not where I live. And Khandra is not my mother. She's a friend." He shook his head. "We're not even the same race." His tone told me he thought it should have been obvious, but it seemed like the perfect opportunity to ask what I had been wondering about him.

"What race are you, exactly?"

He scowled at me. "Have you never seen a dragonborn before? We're not so close to extinction as to be a novelty to someone your age."

Between the pain of the migraine, and being exhausted, I wasn't in a mood to put up with bad manners. I glared back. "Well, I'm not from here. So no, I've never seen a dragonborn before."

I glanced at Gemma, who looked dead on her feet. The poor girl had just had a worse day than any of us. I wanted to find a way to bring her a little comfort, and I needed to sleep off this migraine. I led the girl into the room and pulled back the covers on one side of the bed. "Here Gemma, lay down."

She gently laid her small body on the bed. I tucked her in.

"What do you think you're doing?" Kai demanded.

"We're going to bed." I flopped down on the side opposite Gemma and closed my eyes.

This time, the rumble sounded more like a snarl. "You are not taking my bed."

I peeked at him with one eye, a little worried he was going to attack.

"Then why'd you bring us in here?" My instincts told me I shouldn't show any weakness.

"I was getting a blanket, so you could sleep in the barn."

The barn? Really?

"No, thanks." I snuggled in, draping a protective arm around the little girl. "We're good here."

I hoped he wouldn't call my bluff; because, there was no way I could stop him if he decided to make us move.

Kai growled again and left the room, closing the door behind him.

The tension in my body released, and I smiled slightly. I felt a little bit powerful.

It felt delicious to lie in a bed. Truthfully, I almost cried from the solace. Then I shivered. Nope, I was not going to ruin the coziness by sleeping in damp clothes.

I got up and rummaged through the clothes on the floor. My standards were low; I just wanted something to sleep in that was dry and didn't stink.

I found a large cottony shirt that smelled like pine and musk. The dragonborn was an alluring man even in the scent department. I stripped down and pulled it on. The shirt hit me mid-thigh. *That'll work.*

Gemma's sniffles came from behind me. I turned to see that she was crying. I pulled a second shirt out of the pile and knelt down next to her. Smoothing her hair, I asked if she would like to wear a dry nightgown. Her nod was almost imperceptible.

Once she was dry and settled back into bed, I brushed my fingers lightly over her hair, the way Lyric had always liked when she was small. I began humming a lullaby our mom used to sing to us. Gemma's lip sucked into her mouth as she relaxed. I smiled and thought of Lyric.

The second time through my song, Gemma's breathing became heavy with sleep.

Would she wake up scared in the night? She had been stolen from wherever home was and locked in a cage by goblins, then watched her mother die in a horrifying way. Nightmares seemed like a given.

She didn't wake.

Despite the storm that raged outside, it wasn't long before sleep and I found each other.

SEVEN

Morning came too quickly. Green light shone through the one window in the room like a glaring alarm clock that didn't have a snooze button. I held my hand up to shield my eyes. I woke up sore, tired, and irritated. The dregs of the migraine still lingered from before, along with a very dry mouth.

I had to find Lyric.

How had she fared the storm? Was she worried and scared that I hadn't come last night?

My brain was too stressed to go back to sleep. I got up to look out the window. The crazy thunderstorm had turned to green fog that was so thick I couldn't see anything. With fog that thick, I would have to wait for it to clear before I could hit the road.

Looking over, I saw Gemma was still out cold, her small face covered in filth. The fact that other's were enjoying sleep and I was awake, seemed like an injustice.

If I'm stuck here, I might as well have kept sleeping.

There's probably no coffee in this god-forsaken world, and I am so tired of having a headache all the time.

I want to break something.

I padded my way out of the room in search of a place to pee. Tyler and Kai both snored softly on the floor.

Ugh, they're so irritating!

In a hurry and not sure where to find a bathroom, I stepped outside to go the old-fashioned route. The fog was so dense. If I went far from the house, would I be able to find my way back?

Better not risk it.

I took care of business next to the stairs, cursing said fog for offending my morning with its presence, when I should be going to find my sister. Or at the very least, sleeping and not plagued by any of it.

As soon as I finished, I stepped back inside. I wanted a glass of water and to sleep until it was time to leave this place.

"You know, we have a latrine for a reason." The rumble of Kai's voice startled me.

Are you serious right now?

I was instantly mortified that he'd been aware of what I was doing. So naturally, I scowled at him. "Well, I didn't know where to find it."

"So, at your house, the next option is to use the flower bed out front?" His body was stretched out on the floor, his hands behind his head, like he was relaxing.

"You are so irritating." I could feel my cheeks were flushed.

"You're wearing my shirt." He jerked his chin in the direction of the black t-shirt I wore.

Get me out of this conversation!

I marched to the kitchen area of the large room. There was an old-fashioned sink and pump. I pumped some cool water into my hand and drank, to fix the dry-ass mouth I'd woken up with.

Admittedly, after I had gotten a drink and my mouth felt normal, I was a lot less grumpy. I did, however, still want to go back to sleep, so to avoid more humiliating conversation, I tromped back to bed without a glance in his direction.

My efforts to find sleep again were wasted when Kai showed up and began rifling through his things, making ungodly amounts of noise.

In my head, I told him exactly what I thought about him coming in and being annoying.

There is no reason that he needs to be in here. He's just being rude. What a hateful man.

Being sexy doesn't just give people the right to be inconsiderate.

The poor kid that had been sleeping peacefully next to me got a rude awakening. Her face crumpled like she was going to cry again.

I put a pause on thinking unpleasant thoughts at Kai and put a hand on Gemma's head. "It's okay. We're safe. Go back to sleep."

Gemma's features softened, but she kept wary eyes on the dragonborn.

I whirled around to Kai. "Do you have any manners whatsoever?"

He ignored me and kept pillaging the room. Weapons clanking and rattling as he moved them. My irritation kicked up a notch.

"You can't possibly need to be organizing your crap right now." I hissed.

No response.

I narrowed my eyes at him.

He picked up the goblin knife I had been wearing on my thigh the night before, examining it's black hilt and checking the curved blade for sharpness.

"That is mine," I said. "Can you stay out of my stuff?"

He looked pointedly at the shirt I was wearing—his shirt. "I could have left you in the forest with the Jalak."

Good point.

I glanced at the little girl. She had the covers pulled up to her chin, and her eyes were darting back and forth between us.

"It's okay," I whispered, giving her a small kiss on the forehead. "You're okay."

Kai didn't deserve my snapping at him. I was in a bad mood, but that wasn't his fault. I tried to tamp down my irritation with him as I turned back to face him.

"Okay," I sighed. "You're right. I'm sorry. I will give your shirt back. I just needed something dry to—"

"You're stinking up the entire room." He cut in. "I don't want your apologies. I just want you out of here."

I rocked back, a scowl of outrage on my face.

I take it back.

He deserves all the snapping.

What a prick.

That's when Tyler woke up and started calling out in a panic from the main room. "What's going on? Where am I? Who's there?"

I jumped out of bed to help my friend. "Shh, Tyler, it's okay."

Apparently only his face had woken up. He lay on the stone floor on his back, his breathing quick and shallow. "I can't move! Astrid! What's wrong with me?

I knelt down next to him and put a hand on his shoulder. "You had some kind of tranquilizer dart shot in your neck. I was told the effects take a while to wear off."

"Oh..." He took a calming breath. "Well," His eyes moved back and forth, evaluating. "I guess that explains why I feel so tranquil."

I snorted a single laugh and lightly smacked his shoulder. "I cannot believe you make jokes this early in the morning."

"You know I couldn't feel that, right?" Tyler smiled at me.

I was glad he was back. I even secretly appreciated his humor. It brightened my mood.

Kai took some equipment from his room and went out into the fog. While he was gone, Khandra emerged from her room and started bustling around the kitchen area. I got water for Tyler.

Khandra instructed me to get the fire going while she made breakfast. Since we were here when she didn't want us to be, and since she was hopefully going to feed us, I said, "Yes Ma'am." I didn't tell her I'd never started a fire before. (She seemed like the kind of grandmotherly figure that you don't cross.)

Tyler, unable to move, still lay near the hearth. I discreetly asked him if he knew how to start a fire and could talk me through it.

"Well, if it was a computer or an engine, I could talk you

through it with my eyes closed. But as far as I can tell, you'll want to stack some wood up in there and light it up."

I narrowed my eyes at him. "Not helpful."

"Sorry, the only fireplace I've lit was at my grandma's. It was gas. I just flipped the switch."

I took a few pieces of wood from the bin on the hearth and set them in the fireplace. Then I looked around for matches. I didn't find any.

Am I going to have to rub sticks together here?

I was bumbling around trying to figure out what to do when Kai came in with a basket and an armload of wood. It seemed odd to see Kai, sans all of his weapons, doing something ordinary like chores. The basket he set on the table, and the wood he dumped in the bucket next to me.

"Are you truly this incompetent?" He gestured to the pile of wood in the fireplace.

Rude.

"I'm trying to be helpful." I leaned back and folded my arms.

"Why don't you just use your red magic?" He shrugged out of his jacket.

"I... how did you know about that?"

"I'm a dragonborn. I can smell it." He draped the jacket over a chair at the table.

Not wanting to admit that I didn't know how to use my magic, I looked down. I ran my thumb over my cuff, feeling inadequate.

"Never mind." He practically knocked me over, asserting himself in front of the fire.

"Excuse you!"

He rearranged my perfectly neat stack of firewood into a

disorganized heap and then stretched a hand out toward it. Red light came from his palm and lit the wood instantly.

Oh my gosh, that looks just like my magic.

"You have firepower?" I tried not to sound too interested.

His piercing eyes looked at me flatly. "I'm a dragonborn."

"Right."

A long braid of his dark hair hung down to the middle of his back. I hadn't noticed before. It reminded me of a Viking from a movie.

Warmth from the fire washed over me, and I realized how cold I'd been all morning. Instinctively, I stretched my arms forward to warm my hands.

"Did the Jalak make you wear that?" Kai hooked one finger under the cuff on my arm and gave it a gentle tug before letting his hand drop.

The touch of his callous finger raised the hair on my arm.

"No." I brought my arm to my chest protectively.

His eyebrows pulled together.

"Then why would you wear it?"

Because it's comforting. Because I love it.

"It's none of your business."

He pulled my hand away from my chest to inspect the amber stone imbedded in the worn leather. A shiver ran through me at the contact.

"This kind of magic suppression is government use only." He spoke in a low whisper. "Hard to find, even on the black market."

"What?" My stomach dropped.

No. He's wrong. My mother gave me this. It was special to her.

"Where did you get this?" His eyes searched mine, and his face hardened. "Who sent you?"

I jerked my arm away from him. "What? No one sent me."

I hardly saw him move, and he had a knife at my throat.

"Who sent you?" He growled. His attractive face was suddenly swathed in shadow. Translucent black, claw-tipped wings, adorned with opaque black tribal patterns, unfurled above us. "I won't ask again."

Fear gripped me like it had in the forest. Our faces were suddenly inches apart. My chest began to rise and fall in heated breaths. I could just see the curve of his lips through the shroud of the shadow emanating from him. I couldn't speak.

"Holy giant pair of wings Batman!" Tyler said from where he lay on the floor.

Kai snarled in his direction.

I shuddered.

This is it. He waited for us to get comfortable, and now he's going to kill us.

"What is happening?" Tyler said. "Am I hallucinating?"

"No," Kai said. "But if you impede this interrogation again, you will wish you were only hallucinating."

"Leave him alone," I whispered. Kai's momentary distraction helped me find my voice. "No one sent me." My voice trembled. "I told you, we escaped from the Jalak ship."

"That might have been an elaborate ruse." He pressed the knife against me harder.

"Trust me, buddy," Tyler said. "We wouldn't stink like this if we didn't spend a week on a slave ship with no bathroom and no showers."

"Tyler!" If I could've moved, I would have smacked him.

"If what you say is true," Kai searched my eyes, his nose flaring. "Why would you wear something Lord Alifar created for his personal slaves and spies?"

"Who?"

The shock I felt must have shown on my face, because he eased up a little. "You really didn't know that stone was a magic suppressor." It wasn't a question.

"If I knew this bracelet was going to make people think I'm a spy, why would I openly wear it?"

Kai seemed to consider that for a moment. Then his wings folded up, and the shadows faded away, leaving the attractive, if menacing, human pressed up against me. I held his gaze. Dragonborn was clearly a predator race—it felt important to not yield first, to not show weakness. After a few beats, he backed off and slid his knife into a sheath on the back of his belt.

I wanted to run, but I forced my body to walk to my room, closing the door behind me. Then I sagged against it and let out a shaky breath. The smell of him, and the weapons all around, reminded me that it was Kai's room, not mine. I wished I'd gone anywhere else.

I looked at Gemma, who was sitting on the bed watching me. Her expression was blank. I rubbed my temples as I walked over to sit next to her.

I talked to her, but she remained completely silent. She would move her head in tiny movements to communicate with me, but it seemed she was unwilling to speak. I knew she could speak because I had heard her with her mother.

I played a little guessing game with her and learned a few things about her.

She cried when I asked about her family, and I pulled her into my lap and rocked her for a while.

I had heard of kids refusing to talk when they were traumatized, and I couldn't blame her.

When her crying died down, I asked her if she was hungry, and she nodded.

I didn't want to be in a room with Kai, but I put on a brave front for Gemma. She slipped her tiny hand into mine as we walked, and the gesture nearly broke my heart. I thought about my sister, in a strange land, not knowing where I was. My heart constricted. I hoped she wasn't afraid. I sat Gemma down at the long bench on the side of the table nearest the fire.

Khandra watched us for a moment before turning back to the counter. She poured a small glass of something that resembled orange juice and came over to set it down in front of Gemma.

"I didn't realize last night that you had a child with you." The woman said pointedly to Kai. "I can't believe you let a little girl sleep in such filth. She needs a bath."

She's not the only one...

"Doesn't seem to have done her any harm," Kai said glancing at Gemma.

Khandra tsked and shook her head, turning her attention back to Gemma, her Scottish accent taking on an almost grandmotherly tone. "What's your name?"

Gemma looked at Khandra and then turned to me, eyes wide.

"Her name is Gemma." I put my arm around the girl. "She won't speak."

Khandra didn't seem too concerned with that. She proceeded to ask me questions about Gemma, none of which I could answer. The child tensed with each one.

I finally pulled Khandra aside to where Gemma hopefully couldn't hear us. "All I know is that she was locked in a cage on the Jalak ship. When I got Tyler out, I didn't want to leave her behind, so we brought her along." I glanced over at Gemma and lowered my voice even more. "Her mother died in a horrifying way last night, just before Kai found us."

Khandra put her hand over her mouth, and sadness touched her sharp eyes. "The poor child."

I nodded. "She's six-years-old, likes kittens, and the color purple is her favorite. She has a brother and father somewhere, but when I ask her about her family, she just cries."

The older woman nodded as I spoke, inserting mm's and mm-hmm's here and there.

"That's all I know about her," I finished. "I promised her mother I would get her home."

One swift nod from Khandra. "Set the table."

She walked over to Gemma, abruptly ending our conversation.

I shook my head slightly.

The behavior in this realm leaves much to be desired.

. . .

Khandra coaxed Gemma into a bath before breakfast, in exchange for a biscuit to tide her over, since breakfast wasn't quite ready.

Gemma looked to me with questioning eyes. I nodded my encouragement and told her I would come too. The three of us went into the washroom. It was located off the main room, near the kitchen area. The space was minimal. It was mostly filled with a deep stone basin in the center—large enough to fit two people comfortably. Khandra pumped cold water into the basin for a bath. Then she took a small stone— she called it a heat rock—from a pail in the corner, and placed it in the water. I watched carefully, so I could duplicate the process for myself later. The smooth black rock was the size of a half dollar and looked unimpressive. When the stone hit the water, it glowed red. Not a minute later, steam began rising from the water. I dipped a hand in, the warmth was heavenly.

Fascinating.

Once Gemma was in the bath, she seemed to relax. Since she was in good hands, with her nod of approval, I went to set the table. As I worked, Khandra bustled back and forth from her room to the washroom with clean clothes and supplies.

Eventually, Gemma emerged fresh and clean, wearing a simple red shirt that fell to her knees. A bit of ribbon tied at the waist made it look like a dress. Her hair was brushed and tied back with another length of blue ribbon. She wasn't smiling, but she looked more at ease. She clutched a small stuffed lamb that looked like it had seen better days. I smiled gratefully at Khandra and she waved me off.

"A little healing magic goes a long way."

I raised my eyebrows, curious. Hopefully I'd get the chance to ask about that later.

I bent down to look into Gemma's face. "Did you find a toy?"

The girl nodded slightly.

"Just an old relic from when my son was small," Khandra said. "He dragged that thing everywhere."

She instructed everyone to sit and then served us a meal, akin to biscuits and gravy, that had been baking in a covered pot over the fire.

Sitting at the table next to Kai felt tense. I was half worried he might go into attack-mode again, and half worried about how awful I smelled. I needed a shower, stat. I glanced in his direction, aware of how nice he smelled. He was busy eating and ignoring me.

Good.

I thought I might go crazy stuck in this house with him until the fog cleared. Plus, I was anxious to get to Lyric.

I looked down at the cuff on my arm. Doubt flooded me.

Is this really a magic suppression stone?

Did my mother have magic?

No. I knew her my whole life.

My mother was warm and kind. ...And decidedly normal. She wouldn't give me something designed for slaves. She had worn this cuff herself before she'd passed it on to me.

She must not have known.

Where would she get something like this on Earth?

Kai is wrong. This stone is plain old amber, like my mom said.

I just decided that I was worrying for no reason. In fact,

Kai was such a prick I don't know why I'd even thought twice about what he'd said.

Someone mentioned the fog storm, and my ears perked up.

Khandra was explaining to Gemma, similar to a sand storm in the desert, this was a magic storm. The green color was from trace earth magic mixed with natural gases leaking from a nearby mountain and blowing in from the ocean.

"How long will the fog last?" I asked.

"No one knows," Khandra said. "Last time, it was four or five days."

Panic tightened my insides. *I can't sit around here that long. I have to find Lyric!*

"Is there any way to navigate through it?" I asked.

"Light magic is the only thing strong enough to cut through that." The woman waved her hand.

"Where do we get some of that?"

"You're either born with it, or you're not," she said, then gestured to the lamp on the table. "The rest of us pay for light. And those oil lamps won't get you to the barn in fog this thick."

I felt like screaming.

Why was everything so primitive here when people had magic? But I didn't want to offend these people, so I didn't ask.

Once I finished eating, I helped Tyler eat his food. He cracked a few jokes about it, but I was too distracted to respond.

"Headache?" He asked.

"It's not too bad right now." I shook my head. "I'm just distracted. Sorry..."

"It's okay." He lowered his voice. "Dude, what's with live-action Batman?"

"Kai?" I stole a brief glance at the man in question. "He's a dragonborn." I shrugged. "Which is some kind of race." I raised my voice just above a whisper to add, "He's a class-act jerk."

I hope he really does have super hearing.

Tyler's eyebrows knit together. "And how did we end up here?"

I recounted the events of the night before, along with my worries about finding Lyric.

"No wonder you're distracted," he said. "You should rest."

He was right. But first I planned to take a warm bath.

Not wanting to even be around the dragonborn's clothes, I asked Khandra if I could borrow something to wear. She loaned me a dress. I didn't affront her generosity by asking for something more practical, even though I wanted to.

I'll just wash my clothes and be in my leggings again as soon as possible.

I prepped the bathwater like Khandra had. The red glow of the heat stone intrigued me.

My gaze fell to the stone on my arm, in its setting of brown leather. I rubbed my thumb over it. My thoughts were at war in my head.

This is ridiculous.

I'd always been proud of the fact that I wasn't superstitious or gullible.

But I also didn't believe in magic a week ago.

And Mom had been hiding things from me and Lyric...
Finally, I unlaced the cuff and set it on the corner of the sink.

An experiment.

There was no change. That made sense—I'd taken the cuff off briefly to shower a million times.

After a very long soak in the tub and a triple hair wash, I felt amazing. Not even a trace of headache. I was blissfully warm. The heat stone had kept the bath water a perfect temperature the entire time.

I slipped into the clean dress and braided my wet hair. The cuff on the counter seemed to eye me, as I avoided touching it. Now that the idea had been planted in my mind, it was hard not to link feeling this good to not wearing it. I closed my eyes and took a deep, slow breath.

Timidly, I explored within myself for my magic.

The real test.

It proved easy to find. The moment I brushed against it with my mind, it surged inside of me with such a force that my eyes flew open with a gasp.

I didn't dare mess with my power any further. After what had happened with Brother Miaal, I thought I was likely to destroy the entire room, if not the whole house.

Snatching Kai's shirt off the floor, I used it to grab the cuff, then headed back to his room. Not sure what else to do with the cuff, I carefully hid it in the corner behind a crate full of weapons and gear. I didn't want to risk wearing it, but I didn't know how I could ever part with something that my mother prized so highly. It had been my one treasure for as long as I could remember.

Afterwards, I gathered my and Gemma's dirty clothes and headed back to the bathroom to wash them.

Tyler was trying to chat with Kai, who sat, dressed in dark pants and a black t-shirt, sharpening a battle ax. Gemma, straight-faced and quiet, held tight to her lamb while Khandra explained to the girl how to bake something. No one was aware of the crisis that was happening inside of me. I couldn't believe Kai was right about my cuff. How had I never noticed the difference I felt when I didn't wear it?

I almost never took it off. Mom told me to always wear it. I'd always found such comfort and security in having it on.

I took my stress out on the clothes as I scrubbed the crap out of them.

Who were you mom?
Who am I?

EIGHT

Khandra seemed to decide that Tyler and I weren't spies or enemies after finding out we had saved Gemma. The fact that we were completely ignorant about magic and hailed from the Realm of Stars—her name for our Earth realm—also seemed to factor in.

She wasn't exactly warm, but she'd become a more accommodating hostess. At least, so long as anything we needed didn't take her away from her self-appointed role as Gemma's caretaker. The little girl followed her everywhere, and though she wouldn't speak, Khandra seemed to understand her fine.

Tyler was given a bedroll to make him more comfortable. He couldn't move or feel anything below the neck. Still, it was a nice gesture.

Khandra, being a healer—though according to her, not a very skilled one—took it upon herself to examine his affliction with her magic. But only after her little charge was napping and didn't need her attention for the time being.

Turned out it was a good thing she did, because she

discovered the Jalak had laced the dart with a spell which would keep him immobilized until it was released—which required magic.

"The person with the parry to this spell could easily release the effects," she explained to Tyler. "But I'm going to have to fix you the long way around."

She ordered him to hold still while she worked. I saw him about to say something smart about that, but I gave him a don't-you-dare look and thankfully he kept quiet. I didn't want her to have any reason to change her mind about helping us.

Khandra sat on the stone floor next to Tyler. She took great care to spread her dress around her instead of sitting on it.

She caught me watching her from my perch on a chair nearby. I half expected her to shoo me away, but she simply gestured to her fanned out dress as an explanation, "I need all the help I can get for this one."

"How does sitting like that help you?" I asked.

"Magic comes from the earth itself. When you aren't grounded, you can deplete your magic entirely."

"So you have to touch the stone floor?"

She nodded. "It's a living element that is touching the earth."

I thought back to the Jalak cell. "What about wood?"

"Living wood is living—still connected to the earth. Dead wood is useless."

The only magic exposure I'd had so far had been pretty unpleasant, so watching her heal was captivating.

She closed her eyes and hummed softly, a tune that was

foreign and haunting. Her hands danced in a slow, rhythmic flow, hovering over Tyler's body.

When her eyes fluttered open, she seemed to put all of her focus on her hands, which she held several inches apart.

An orb of translucent orange light grew between her open palms. She turned it over in her hands several times before carefully placing it on Tyler's sternum. Then she whispered words, in a language I didn't understand, and used one flat hand to push the orb into his body. Tyler inhaled sharply. Luckily, he couldn't move. It made him a model patient.

Khandra repeated the ritual over each joint in his body. It was tedious. I understood why she needed to be grounded to use that much magic.

Eventually, she leaned back, sweat glistening on her forehead. "It will take time." She was breathing hard. "But by the time this fog clears, you'll be able to go find your friends together."

"Are you trying to get rid of us?" Tyler said in mock sadness.

"All guests have a limit to their being welcome. Uninvited ones more so than the rest."

Tell us how you really feel about it.

Khandra fanned her face with her hands.

"Do you need some water?" I asked her.

She nodded, and I hurried to get some. When I handed her the drink, I asked, "How do you control how much magic you use at one time?"

After downing the entire glass of water, she said, "It all starts in the mind. You must stay calm and focused to control the magic."

That made sense to me. In the slave quarters, I had struggled to find the magic even with a lot of concentration.

Though I had put my cuff back on just before that. Maybe that explained why I could hardly find the magic, and there were only the dregs of power compared to the first time I'd used it.

"Can you teach me?" I asked.

"What color is your magic?"

"I've only used it twice. Both times it looked red."

The woman shook her head. "Better to ask Kai. Dragonborn are often skilled with red magic, him more than most."

Yeah, I'll ask him right after he bites my head off next time.

I tried a different approach. "I would be so grateful if you would teach me anything you can about the mind stuff."

Khandra acted annoyed but explained a few things anyway. I chose to take it as a sign that she was flattered that I wanted her expertise.

The main idea was to put your mind in the right state. Breathing and grounding helped, and many people connected their state to a calming trigger. For Khandra, it was a lullaby native to her people, often sung by her mother.

Each color of magic was accessed at a different place in the body. When she described the locations and the colors, it sounded like the seven chakras chart we had back on Earth. The colors of the rainbow starting with red—fire and all its subsidiaries—at the base of the core.

No wonder I'm not cold since I have my cuff off. I've got a magic heat source in me.

Healing—orange—came from the sacrum. Yellow—air

manipulation—being at the solar plexus. Followed by earth —green, and water—blue, each at the heart and throat, respectively.

"The magic that comes from the crown is light magic." She nodded like that was the end of that. According to the chakra chart I'd been mentally following, she had either skipped one, or people on earth had made up an extra.

Touching the space between my eyebrows, I asked, "Is there magic here?"

Khandra narrowed her eyes and spoke, her voice laced with disgust. "There's only one person to ever have magic of that color." She turned and spat on the floor.

Ope, I guess I shouldn't ask. It must've been a bad person.

"Hey, look!" Tyler waved his arms at us. "My arms work! They're a little tingly, but I'm thawing out from the top down, like a popsicle."

"That's great!" I smiled. Khandra simply hauled herself up and walked away, saying something about making a decent dress for Gemma.

"Soon you can clean the stink off of you." Kai said from across the room.

I whispered, so Kai wouldn't know I agreed with something he'd said. "He's not wrong." I wrinkled my nose but softened it with an apologetic shrug.

"Believe me, I know." Tyler raised his eyebrows in emphasis. "I'd be chasing myself out of the room... only I can't get away."

We both laughed. It felt good to release some tension.

"Here's what I can't figure out," Tyler said. "How did Kai know to come help us in the woods last night?"

I shrugged, not particularly concerned about the answer.

I was just glad he'd had a lapse in his egocentric personality and helped us.

"I was coming back from a job and smelled Jalak scum," Kai said, standing and heading toward the door. "Hard to resist the lure of easy prey after a hard day's work."

"So you have a personal vendetta against the Jalak?" Tyler asked.

"Not your business." Kai growled as he left the house. This time, the door closed with a good deal of force.

"Don't break my doors, Kai Hjelmstad." Khandra said from her chair by the fire, where she was rummaging through a basket of material.

"Aren't you worried he'll get lost out in the fog?" Tyler asked.

I didn't think I could find it in my heart to be sad if he didn't come back.

"His senses are keen. He doesn't need to see to find his way," she said.

That's unfortunate.

"So, Kai and the Jalak... is it a race rivalry? Or..." Tyler trailed off.

"The Jalak Brotherhood stole his mate and sold her as a slave," Khandra said, smoothing a soft blue fabric across her lap. "When he found her, it was too late. Her new master had beaten her to death."

That's horrible!

I pressed a hand to my heart, glad Lyric had escaped the slavers. I shuddered, thinking of Gemma and the rest of the prisoners who might have faced a similar fate.

"Wow," Tyler breathed.

"Hmm... Worst part was, she was with child when they took her." Khandra shook her head.

Okay, I could see why Kai had some anger issues. Though I still wasn't about to trust him or his knives.

"Dragonborn offspring are scarce as it is." Khandra threaded a needle as she continued. "A shame to lose one with such good breeding."

Ope.

I shifted in my seat. My ears and neck suddenly feeling very warm.

Kai is a gorgeous specimen—built by the gods even. But do we need to discuss his breeding?

"No wonder the guy looks angry." Tyler frowned.

Khandra nodded. "Been a lost soul all the years since."

Can we please change the subject?

I cleared my throat. "Why doesn't your government stop the Jalak from trafficking slaves?"

She bristled. "Lord Alifar and his court buy from the Jalak more often than most."

Disgust filled me.

Just like Lyric. People being taken from their families. The thought of such corruption and rampant disregard for people's lives made me angry. But I was stuck here in this cottage with no power to do anything about it, including find my sister.

Tyler took advantage of Khandra's willingness to chat while she cut and sewed. He asked questions about the realm, and Kai, and her family.

Kai was close friends with Khandra's son, Ryder. Which brought him to stay occasionally.

"Ryder doesn't like me here alone," Khandra rolled her

eyes. "When he does a supply run for the farm, he has Kai come stay at the house."

It seemed strange that the frightening dragonborn had such an ordinary life with ordinary friends. Or was civil enough to want to help around their farm. But who was I to question the inner workings of a moody male? I didn't think I would forgive him for how he'd treated me, but I couldn't really fault him for being sullen after losing his wife and kid. I couldn't imagine losing Lyric.

"Is that where your son is now, getting supplies in town?" Tyler asked.

She nodded. "Didn't realize he'd have to hunker down there for a storm. Kai was off on one of those jobs, so he didn't get here in time to warn him." She'd said 'those jobs' in a tone that gave the impression she didn't approve of Kai's line of work.

My mind instantly volunteered several shady things the dragonborn might be involved with.

Thanks brain, I don't know how I'd manage without you.

But it was Tyler who had the guts to straight-up ask about it. It slightly mortified me.

Still, I checked my cuticle beds with my ears perked.

"With no cause of his own to care about, he works as a contractor."

That's informative. How boring.

Tyler moved his arm. "What does he contract?"

Thank you, Tyler.

He was on a roll with his snooping.

Khandra shook her head, "I cannot speak it." She kissed her knuckles, then pressed them to her opposite collarbone. I got the impression it was a gesture of reverence—like making the sign of the cross. "I just pray for his soul."

"So, should we be worried that he's going to kill us all?" I was only half joking, thinking of all the weapons in his room.

"Oh, no. He only does that when he's paid to do it."

Great. That's not very comforting.

"So, he's an assassin!" Tyler was clearly impressed and his joints were beginning to work, as he gestured with both of his hands.

"Tyler, being an assassin is not cool," I said, trying to emphasize my point with my face.

"You're right." He nodded. "It's not cool... It's awesome!"

Oh, brother.

I rolled my eyes, and Tyler leaned up on his elbows. "Think about it, Astrid! We could hire him to help us."

"What?" I jerked my head back. "No way! Who the heck do we need to kill?"

"Not kill. Protect."

I shook my head. "Hard pass."

"Hear me out." He moved his leg and gasped. "Did you see that?"

"You're not distracting me. The answer is no."

He began ticking off on his fingers. "The Jalak are looking for us. He could keep us safe. He's from here, so he knows his way around. That alone would save a ton of time!"

I was still shaking my head no.

Tyler raised his voice—something I'd never heard him do. "Lyric needs us—I'm sick of sitting around waiting and worrying! I don't want to fumble our way to finding her or risk something horrible happening."

His sudden passion surprised me. "Do you think I want to wait around here? I'm going crazy! The only reason we separated was to save you!"

"Shh!" Khandra waved her arms. "The child needs rest. I don't want you two waking her!"

Gemma. Another responsibility I hadn't meant to pick up along the way.

How am I supposed to take care of everyone?

"I'm not asking for your permission." Tyler said, stone-faced.

"She is *my* sister."

"She's the love of my life."

My whole body tensed. I'd never heard him declare it so boldly before. I didn't like it.

Possessiveness flared in my gut. I knew it was selfish. Someday she would grow up and live her own life.

But not yet. And not for some teenage romance.

I can't lose Lyric.

I headed to Kai's room, suddenly wanting to be alone. I flopped down on my back on the bed and closed my eyes.

I distracted myself by making a mental checklist of what needed to be done the moment that damned fog cleared. The list was short.

One. Gather everything I brought with me.

The clothes on my back, the cuff hidden in the corner, and Tyler's motorcycle key that had somehow survived in the pocket of my leggings.

Two. Leave.

Lyric and Ro wouldn't have stayed at the rendezvous

point for long. They would have had to find shelter in the storm.

No one else can travel in this fog either. They won't be too far ahead of us.

I stayed alone in that room for hours, until I felt more rational. I flopped my arm over my eyes and thought about Khandra's healing magic. It was so serene. If only my magic wasn't so destructive.

I mean, it would be good in a fight for my life, if I knew how to use it. But how handy is it going to be on the daily?

Until this whole disaster, the number of to-the-death fights I'd been in had been exactly zero.

I practiced calming my mind. Breathing deeply. Then I kicked off my tennis shoes and planted my feet on the cool stone floor, letting myself get grounded.

Picturing the location of the root chakra on the chart in my mind's eye, I sent my awareness to the deepest part of my core. There it was. My magic.

Though my eyes were closed, I could see it there. It glowed bright red and flickered. It seemed to mock me, eager to have me call it into the world.

What a strange thing to feel the power that's mine. A part of me, yet separate.

Thinking of Lyric's CFS, I wished I had power like the healer instead.

I mentally traveled up my body to where she had talked about her healing magic living. I imagined an orange glow living there, that I could partner with and use to heal my sister, so that she would never again need her chair.

As I mentally searched my abdomen, I saw a flicker of orange light. My eyes flew open, and I sat up.

Heartbeat quickening, I glanced around. No one would see what I was about to try.

I sat cross-legged on the ground, and flared my borrowed dress out around me, as Khandra had done. The cool of the stone against my legs felt soothing. Placing both of my palms on my belly, I breathed slow and deep. I sensed the orange light in my core. A smile touched my lips. This magic wanted to play.

I invited it to come through me. The orange magic burst out through my hands and into every corner of the room. There was no orb, only chaos. Orange light undulated all around, filling the space with swirls and waves.

A single sound, like light laughter, escaped me. I was so surprised by it. I caught my bottom lip between my teeth. In the room's privacy, my smile of delight could not be contained. I set it free. It felt so good to lower my guard.

Raising my palms to the heavens and stretching my arms high, I closed my eyes and basked in joy—a feeling I hadn't experienced in a very, very long time.

The door banged open and startled me out of my reverie. My head whipped around. Kai's large frame filled the doorway.

The look on his face told me he wasn't any more excited to see me than I was to see him.

I scrambled up from my place on the floor. "Ever heard of knocking?" Self-conscious, I waved at the orange light in the room that was lingering like a stray dog with nowhere to go.

"It's my room."

"But I'm staying here, so you should have the decency to knock."

"I thought you said your magic was red." He nodded pointedly at the orange light filling the room.

"Why do you care?" I shrugged.

His low growl accompanied his words. "Because I don't like being lied to."

I folded my arms protectively over my stomach but raised my chin in an attempt to show strength. "I didn't lie."

"This isn't red magic." He leaned in with a challenging glare.

Obviously.

"Well, I didn't know I had orange magic."

And I'd like to get back to being excited about it, you buzzkill.

Kai made a small rumbling sound. "So, you don't need my help with red magic, then." He brushed past me into the room.

"Wait." I turned to face him again. "You were going to help me?"

"Khandra can help you with that." He gestured toward the healing magic that had mostly faded away.

"But she said my red magic..."

The magic that terrifies me.

His shoulders stiffened. "You have two colors?"

I hesitated. "Is that bad?"

"It..." He thought about it for longer than I liked. "It's very rare."

"Okay, but not bad?"

"I guess that depends on if you're trustworthy."

"Well, what about you? You have those dragon wings you can whip out at any moment—that's magic. And you also have red magic. So why is it weird for me to have two things?"

"Light magic is just one form of magic. Different races have different abilities. But the elemental powers never manifest more than one at a time."

"You mean, rarely?"

Kai narrowed his eyes at me. "Show me."

"You just saw the healing magic." I gestured around the room where the orange light had been before.

"Yes." He inclined his head towards me. "Now I want to see the fire."

I took a small step back, shaking my head. "No way."

"So you're lying?"

"No." I swallowed. "I'm protecting you." *That came out wrong.* I rushed on. "And everyone else in this house."

He cocked his scarred eyebrow at me and folded his powerful arms.

"It's not... I can't control it." My voice lowered to a whisper. "Last time I let that magic out, I killed three Jalak."

Kai smiled wickedly. He was terrifying and gorgeous.

My gaze was drawn to his mouth. I looked away quickly.

Keep your head, Astrid.

I was surprised he didn't say something rude. I hated confessing my weakness to him, of all people.

He began filling a travel pack with supplies. "Get ready to go."

"Is the fog cleared?" I looked through the window—it still looked green to me—then did a double take. "Wait. Where are *you* going?"

"Tyler hired my services."

Irritation flashed through me.

That little...

I rushed out of the room to find him.

While I'd been hiding in the other room, Tyler had gotten full function of his body back.

Good. Because I'm about to pummel him.

I found him in the washroom, brushing his freshly washed hair out with his fingers. He was in clothes that he must have borrowed from Ryder's closet, because nothing he was wearing would have stretched over the dragonborn's muscular frame.

I propped my hands on my hips. "You hired that prick to come with us?"

"I told you I was going to." His tone was nonchalant as he smoothed a stray red lock of hair off his forehead.

I gritted my teeth. "I told you I didn't want him around."

"Astrid." He turned to look at me, his expression determined. "The guy can sense his way through the fog, so we can leave now instead of waiting for the storm to clear."

Okay, that alone might be worth the price of having to put up with the dragonborn.

Tyler saw my hesitation and grinned. "I told you it was a good idea."

I folded my arms, shifting my weight to the side. "Well, how are we going to pay him?"

Tyler glanced around before leaning in to whisper. "I told him I have a lot of money in savings on Earth."

I rolled my eyes. "And he is just going to help us, on your promise of money in a different realm?"

What an idiot.

"Not exactly..." He gave me a sheepish look.

"Well?"

"He said he would take your cuff as payment." Tyler scuffed his hand through his red hair.

Anger roiled in me. "You were just going to steal my mother's cuff?" I shoved against his shoulders. "It isn't yours to give away."

"I was going to talk to you about it."

I started towards him. "You lying, thieving..."

He winced, standing his ground. "It's to find Lyric!" he blurted.

I stopped. His face was pale behind his freckles.

I was still seething. "I can find her without Kai. ...Or you."

"Astrid, listen to yourself." He placed a gentle hand on each of my shoulders and looked down into my face. "Your mom would not want you to go out there on a dangerous journey alone just to keep her cuff."

Tyler had a point, yet I pulled away from him. "You don't know what my mother would want."

"But you do." I could tell his tone was meant to be reassuring, but it struck a different chord.

My shoulders fell. "I don't know if I do." All my anger deflated, replaced by sadness. "She left me with more questions than answers."

And the burden of taking care of everything and keeping Lyric safe.

Tyler's lanky arms wrapped around me in a hug. "Let's just go find Lyric. We can figure the rest out later."

After a beat, I hugged him back. "Sorry I pushed you."

He patted my head. "Astrid, you're too miniature to do any real damage."

I pulled back and elbowed him hard in the gut.

Tyler sucked in a breath. "I changed my mind. Enemies will fall, never having seen your elbows coming."

NINE

It wasn't long before we were all ready to go. After tying my cuff on Tyler's wrist for safekeeping, since it wouldn't affect him, I relayed the directions to the rendezvous point. Well, as far as I remembered them from the map I'd lost. Kai seemed to think he knew the place.

At Khandra's insistence, we left Gemma in her care until it was time to portal-travel home. Gemma seemed pleased with the arrangement, and I was happy to know she would be safe there.

I was back in my own clothes. Kai had strapped Tyler with a pack full of gear, and the already intimidating dragonborn wore enough weapons and combat gear to outfit a small platoon. What kind of battle was he expecting on this errand? I couldn't picture anyone challenging him.

Hopefully, just a precaution.

The fog was thick. We tethered a line between us, with Tyler bringing up the rear, leaving me in the middle.

Kai's dragon sight—an ability that allowed him to see through any magic illusion—let him see past the magic storm pretty well.

All I could see was green. I didn't know how long or how far we walked, but it felt like hours. Sometimes weaving around, sometimes walking straight.

We kept quiet, though I didn't think anyone else would be insane enough to be out in this. If you've never walked through fog or darkness so thick that you can't even look down and see your body, let me tell you, it's unnerving. Enough to make a person feel like they're going crazy. It almost felt like I was alone except that I could feel the tug of the rope that linked me to the others.

Eventually, Kai led us into a building. A mixture of spices hung in the air, and the aroma made my tongue tingle.

"This is it," Kai said.

It took a moment for my eyes to adjust to seeing things again. Kai lifted one hand. Red light swirled up and gathered the green mist that had come in the door with us, incinerating it in a crimson flash. The room was lit with lamps and filled with rows of bins that contained sacks and jars. A spice shop. Kai rang the bell on the counter. The weathered face of a man peeked out from behind the door that led to what I guessed was a back room.

"Can I help you?"

"We are looking for a female that may have sheltered here for the storm," Kai said.

The man's eyes darted between the members of our group. "I don't know what you're doing out in this storm, but if you're not here to buy spice, I can't help you." He retreated and closed the door.

Without warning, Kai unhooked the line that connected him to me and let it drop as he hopped over the counter and burst through the door to the back room.

What's happening? Did he sense something?

Imagining my sister trapped in the back room, I rushed around the counter, dragging Tyler with me. If Lyric was back there, I wanted to see for myself. I almost knocked into Kai when I entered the room. Tyler did knock into me.

Several people stood in the small room, nervously watching our trio. The plump older man who had peeked through the door stood protectively in front of two women. One with an infant in her arms, and one with gray in her hair.

No sign of Lyric. My shoulders fell.

The spice merchant spoke. "We are under the protection of High Lord Alifar. If you think you can come in and threaten my family—"

"We're not going to hurt you." I spoke with my hands up in what I hoped was a universally understood, we-come-in-peace gesture.

"We're trying to find my sister." I inched forward, looking into their faces. "She's tall. She has blond hair and bright silver eyes—you'd remember if you saw them."

The strangers stole glances at each other but said nothing.

"They know something," Tyler said into my ear.

"Please." I tried again. "It's really important. She was hiding with a... man." I hesitated on the last word. Since Ro was a shapeshifter, I didn't know what disguise he would have chosen.

"She came here after the ship docked." The older woman nodded. "But they left before the storm came in."

My body relaxed a bit. She had made it to the rendezvous point.

Did they head to the rebel base with the storm coming?

For the millionth time, I wished that our phones worked, so I could just call her.

"Did you see who she left with?" Tyler asked.

Good question.

"It was just her and one of the Jalak Brotherhood," the woman said.

I froze.

"Crap," Tyler said.

Don't jump to conclusions, Astrid.

I took a breath and tried to think logically.

"It might have been Ro," I said to Tyler, then turned back to the family. "Did she go willingly?"

The younger woman tapped the shoulder of the older woman and whispered something. The elder nodded.

"Are you Astrid?" The younger woman asked.

"Yes!"

The older woman stepped over to a small desk and pulled something out of the drawer. She held out a folded piece of paper. Kai moved to retrieve it, but the woman pulled it back. "Not you. This is for the girl."

I walked, still tethered to Tyler, who bumped along behind me.

"Thank you," I said. Hungrily unfolding the paper with Lyric's handwriting.

Astrid,

I saw you jump off the ship. So cool! I didn't think you would ever do something like that!

Ro says we can't wait anymore. We're going to meet up with his friends. Don't worry about me. (I know you are.) Everything is good. On to Plan B.

Love,

Lyric

P.S. Did you notice how amazing it feels here? It's like their earth is alive on a whole new level! I even feel stronger here.

What if we could bring some magic back to our earth when we go? I'm going to find out. Hurry and catch up with us. I can't wait to see you!

Tyler was reading over my shoulder. "What's Plan B?"

Smiling, I hugged the letter to my chest. "I know where they're headed."

I turned to the guys. "They've gone to the rebel base."

Growling, Kai took my arm and dragged us out to the spice room again. Someone closed the door and quickly latched it behind us.

"What is your deal? Let go!" I jerked my arm, but he held firm.

Kai got right in my face. "How am I supposed to keep

you alive when you walk around saying things that could get you killed?"

My heart beat quickened, his grip on my arm heating my skin. He was so intense. I wanted to growl back at him.

His grip on my arm loosened just slightly. "If these Alifar loyalists think you are in league with rebels, they could bring the government down on us."

"But they wouldn't because you're terrifying, and we're with you," Tyler said confidently.

Kai glanced at Tyler. "I do not contract work that directly opposes Lord Alifar." The dragonborn narrowed his piercing gray eyes. "If he becomes your enemy, you're on your own."

"Okay." I wrenched my arm and Kai finally released his grip. "But we're just going to the rebel base to get Lyric and leaving. We're not teaming up with them. Ro is the one who has friends there."

"You'll take us that far, right?" Tyler asked. "Because the contract is for you to help us find Lyric."

Kai looked at me. "Did you say your sister has silver eyes?"

"Yeah..." I glanced at Tyler.

What does he care?

"She's special," Tyler added. "One of a kind."

"No kidding." Kai tilted his jaw in emphasis.

My stomach tightened. My head felt too warm.

He'd better not be getting any ideas about Lyric.

She's not even sixteen years old.

Kai moved on, oblivious to my sudden rankling. "You said you know where they are?"

I swallowed the bitterness that had reared inside of me.

"Yes. Ro told me how to get there." I paused to refocus my thoughts. "Just... let me think for a second." Closing my eyes, I searched my memory.

"Here," Kai said, looking through the rows of spices, until he found what he wanted. He came back with a grayish leaf. "Chew on this."

"What will it do to me?"

"Sage clears the mind," He said. "Khandra would make a tea, but chewing on it will work."

Warily, I put the dried leaf in my mouth and chewed. A familiar flavor bloomed on my tongue, a spice my mom used when she'd made chicken soup. As I chewed, I closed my eyes again and tried to remember what Ro had said. The memory did seem a little clearer.

I relayed the directions as I remembered them. "Twenty kilometers directly south of Death's Gate, there's a well. East from the well two kilometers lies a fork in the path. Take the left branch and continue to the stream. Follow that upstream to the waterfall. Behind the waterfall is a cave."

Kai grumbled his irritation.

I guessed this job was turning out to be more time consuming than he'd thought.

"How do we find Death's Gate?" Tyler asked.

"Is it far?" I asked.

"Death's Gate is two days' walk from here."

"How far does this storm reach?" I dreaded walking in the green mist again. I didn't think I could stay sane if we had to endure it for two days.

"I do not know, but the air often changes on the far side of this valley." Kai hooked the tether back to his belt, leading us outside without another word.

. . .

We walked for a while before the fog began to dissipate. Though everything had a green haze for a while longer, I could finally see through it. The landscape reminded me of Arizona. We'd lived there for a while when Lyric was small. Mostly red dirt with brush and cacti.

We trudged up an incline, and my legs felt the burn. Once we got high enough, it was incredible to look back over the valley. The basin was filled with thick green mist. Beyond the mist were forested mountains on the other side of the valley, a stark contrast to the desert on this side. To one side was the ocean, to the other side were plains that stretched into hills and more forest. The line between green and brown wasn't gradual. It was colorful and vibrant until it wasn't, almost as though someone had poured herbicide on this entire mountain.

Kai kept us moving. I thought I might pass out by the time we reached the top of the mountain and he finally allowed us to rest. Parched, and shaking from the workout that my body thought was cruel and unusual punishment, I collapsed onto my butt in the dirt. The sun in this realm was glaring.

Kai grabbed a cactus with his bare hands and burned the spines off with a wave of crimson light. Unsheathing a knife, he skinned the thing and then chopped the green meat into chunks. He handed me a few chunks and tossed one in his mouth.

I took a bite. It was juicy, like a watermelon, but not sweet. It reminded me of a cucumber. There was a grittiness to it that felt like sand in my teeth, which I didn't like, but I was grateful for the sustenance.

After Tyler ate a few pieces, he broke the silence.

"This is taking forever. Isn't there a faster way to travel in this realm than walking?"

When the assassin didn't answer, Tyler tried again. "Don't you have cars, or planes, or anything? How can we possibly walk for two days? It's unbelievable. What I wouldn't give for my motorcycle right now."

Tyler chewed on another piece of cactus.

"Speaking of which." He touched my arm. "Astrid, I am crazy impressed that you rode my bike! No one even forced you! Wasn't it so awesome? You left her in a safe place, right?"

I filled my mouth with a huge bite of cactus to avoid responding. I had shoved the bike into a crop of bushes. It had rolled a bit and was probably going to be very hard to get back out and up the hill. But the upshot was that probably no one would see it from the road? I was sure it had a few new scratches.

Especially since I dropped it.

"Astrid?" Tyler leaned in to peer at my face. "Seriously, she's safe, right?"

I swallowed. "Yeah... She's safe."

"Oh, good!" Tyler looked genuinely relieved, and I felt a shot of guilt.

It better still be there when we get back. I couldn't afford to buy him another one.

We began walking again. Thankfully, we didn't need to be tethered anymore, so I walked several paces away from the dragonborn. Being near him was more than I wanted to deal with right now.

A few minutes later, Tyler pressed Kai again. "Does everyone just walk everywhere? People have magic. It seems like you should be way more advanced than we are on earth."

"People on your earth use technology. People on here use magic." He shrugged. "It's just different. People in your realm are very disconnected from the earth."

I scoffed inwardly at his judgy comment.

"Have you been there?" Tyler sounded genuinely interested.

Kai nodded.

"What brought you to our realm?" Tyler asked.

"My Special Ops team was stationed there. Reconnaissance," Kai said.

Tyler nodded. "Oh, you're military?"

"Ex-military."

"Did you ride a motorcycle when you were there? It's like flying."

"Tyler, he has wings," I pointed out. "Besides, I think he's the type that isn't impressed by... anything."

Out of the corner of my eye, I saw Kai glance over, but I ignored him.

"People with yellow light magic ride the wind here," Kai said to Tyler. "Those who have no wings or wind magic pay for wind stones that can make a vessel glide over the earth."

"Great." Tyler clapped once. "Let's do that."

Kai gestured around at our barren surroundings. "How do you plan to pay for a wind stone or a vessel?"

"You're a criminal." Tyler shrugged. "Why don't you just steal one?"

"I am an assassin, not a thief." Kai shook his head like that should have been obvious.

"Apparently that gives you some kind of moral high-ground?" I said it under my breath, several yards away, but Kai threw me an icy look that told me he'd heard me.

Good.

No matter his tragic history, he needed to check his egotistical attitude. We've all been through stuff.

"Dude, your wings are huge! You could fly and carry us! Eh, buddy?" Tyler slung his arm around Kai's shoulder. The dragonborn had him on the ground so fast, I didn't see exactly what happened.

"Do not touch me." Kai growled.

"Got it." Tyler swallowed hard.

The assassin stood. "And I do not carry anyone."

Tyler got up and dusted himself off. "No problem."

It was hours later when we stopped for the night next to a stream. A few trees and a grassy hill secluded the place Kai chose for camping. He made a small fire and then stalked away, saying he would be back.

Having the assassin gone, I breathed out tension I hadn't realized I'd been carrying all day.

"Maybe once we find Death's Gate, we can do the rest without him?" I kicked off my shoes.

"No way. He's not getting paid until we find Lyric," Tyler said, touching the cuff.

It was worth a shot.

Kai wasn't gone long. When he came back, he marched over and ordered me to follow him.

"Not unless we're going to get a foot massage." When I

didn't jump up and salute his request, he hauled me up by my arm and dragged me with him.

"Let go!" I pulled against him, but it was like fighting with a one-ton truck.

"Should I come too?" Tyler stood.

Kai growled at him. Tyler sat back down.

The assassin led me around until we came to a clearing where a large black dome shimmered in the center.

"What is that?" I recoiled.

"A training circle." He pulled me toward it.

Reluctantly, I stepped with him through the barrier. We were swallowed by darkness, and I could see exactly nothing. Only then did he release my arm.

I clutched my hands and spun around, trying to find something, anything to orient me.

"Ugh! You're such a bully," I said through my bared teeth. "I hate you!"

Through the pitch black, I heard him chuckle.

Fire magic blazed in my core, begging to be released. I whirled around trying to find the dragonborn, but it was an endless sea of nothing. Worse than walking in the green fog. My bare feet crunched on what I hoped were leaves and rocks, though my brain was trying desperately to convince me that there was something more sinister than that underfoot.

No. I will not show weakness.

The deep rumbling of Kai's voice came from behind me. "Bring out your fire."

"I won't give you the satisfaction."

"Light up the space."

My breathing became more and more shallow, as fear

gripped me. Anxiety rising in my veins. I was on the edge of a panic attack.

I turned in a circle again. A small red flame just a couple of yards away revealed the man who had cast the light. The light grew and snaked around me several times, cocooning me in a spiral of red light. Warmth enveloped me, and I allowed the relief to sink in and calm my panicked heart.

"If you cannot control your mind, you will never control your magic."

He stepped closer. Then he dropped his hand, and all the light was snuffed out.

In my mind, I could see the magic in me that was fully charged and raring to be released.

If I destroy anything, it's on Kai. He asked for this.

Tentatively, I reached inside and tapped my red magic. It flowed out of me like a burst dam. There was no controlling it. I brought my hands up as if to shield myself from the fragments of shattered earth that might come back at me. Everything around me was consumed in flames. It incinerated everything inside the dome on every side of me. I was in the center of the inferno, my limbs shaking.

I'm burning alive!

Dropping to the ground, I threw my arms around my head to shield from the raging fire.

When the flames died away, and I realized I was still alive, I looked at my arms and hands. Not even pink from a burn. Then I winced. There was way too much skin. My clothes had burned away. Crap! I wrapped my arms around myself.

Within the dome, the earth was black and charred. Only

a few embers remained. The darkness was gone. Light shone through the shimmery surface of the barrier.

Kai stared down at me from across the circle wearing a shocked expression and all of his clothes.

I felt my cheeks heat with embarrassment and anger. He had pushed me to light up. When our eyes locked, it seemed to jolt him. He shrugged his jacket off, then peeled off his black v-neck shirt and handed it to me. He turned to give me privacy as I pulled it on. It hung to my thighs and smelled like Kai. While he was turned away, I examined his broad shoulders and powerful back. A tribal tattoo wrapped his upper left arm and shoulder, snaking around to his chest. His skin held a few scars, but no sign of his wings. He looked human. He looked... incredible. Which was irritating because he was a real jerk.

I cleared my throat. When he turned to face me, I looked away, gesturing at the destruction I'd just caused. "I told you I couldn't control it."

"You incinerated the dark spell within the circle. I'm actually surprised."

I wanted to fireball him in the face and see how surprised he was then. *I'm so done with this.*

Pivoting, I strode to the edge of the dome and tried to walk through, but my body hit something solid.

"How do I get out of this... thing?" I looked around for the origin of the field.

It was being projected by three small discs on the ground. The most high-tech looking equipment I'd seen since leaving earth.

"It's a training circle. Standard military use for dangerous weapon or magic training."

"Right," I snapped. "So how do I get out of it?"

"I thought you wanted to train."

I glowered at the shirtless dragonborn. "I would rather die than train with you."

"You can earn the right to leave by doing some drills."

"You're holding me captive to train with you?" I folded my arms. "I'm not dressed for training."

"Yeah, you put on quite a show," He said with a cocky half smile.

"Ugh," I glared at him. "You're revolting."

He chuckled once. "With the amount of power that you just displayed, you're a danger to everyone around you unless you learn some discipline."

"Oh, now you're scared of me?"

"I am not afraid. It's foolish to leave you untrained when you're so volatile. There's a difference."

"First off..." I cocked my fists on my hips. "I'm a very disciplined person. And second, I am not volatile."

"Says the woman who just lost it when she couldn't have her way."

"What?" I stepped up to him. "I was not throwing a tantrum. I was having a panic attack!"

"Mmm. Volatile." The way his hair brushed his well-built shoulders when he nodded—so sure of himself—inflamed my anger.

"What'd you expect?" I shoved against his immovable chest. "You dragged me here, against my will." I grew more intense with each point. "You tossed me in a dark abyss, preying on my fears. You expect me to fend for myself, when I have no clue where I am or what I need to do!" I shoved at him again. "I don't know where I am, and horrible things keep happening. Why am I the one who has to always be in control, always take care of everything and everyone?" I shoved him a third time. He still didn't move. "Keep it together Astrid. Show no weakness. Everyone needs your strength. Fall in line! Sacrifice everything. Protect her at all costs. How could you just leave me alone to carry all of that?" I stopped. My breathing heavy.

Kai's scarred eyebrow was cocked, and he gave a low, rumbling growl.

Nice going, Astrid. I broke eye contact, looking anywhere but his piercing gaze.

He is such an asshole. Of course he's annoyed with emotions.

What did I expect? An apology for his rude behavior?

What happened to my show-no-weakness plan?

After a bout of punishing silence, Kai said, "Are you ready to begin?"

I rolled my eyes and turned to face him.

"Fine. Let's get this over with."

Better to stay and show strength, than to leave like a coward.

He nodded and held out his hands—an invitation.

"What? Hold hands? No thanks."

Not interested in physical contact.

My eyes strayed to his bare bronzed chest as if challenging my own convictions.

I reminded myself that he was a bully.

"You're going to use red power on me," he said. "Touching skin is easiest."

I froze, remembering Brother Miaal incinerated on the floor in my cell.

Kai raised an eyebrow. "If you don't want to use hands, I

can get more creative."

"Ew. No." I slapped my hands into his. "If something bad happens, just remember I warned you that I'm dangerous."

He gave a little smile. "Not to me you're not."

We'll see about that.

"Ready?" His thumbs brushed once across the backs of my hands. The gesture sent a tingle through me, slowing my sense of time. My gaze fell to the three scars that crossed his chiseled abs.

So, he's attractive and not wearing a shirt. Chill, Astrid.

Annoyed at my body's reaction, I cleared my throat and nodded my head.

After my outburst of magic, I was surprised to find that I had red light left to draw on. Being grounded really made a huge difference. When I searched, there it was, deep in my core.

Kai instructed me to concentrate and compel the magic to become an extension of myself.

"If you and your magic are divided because you're afraid of the power, you will lose control."

That's not vague at all.

"How am I supposed to compel it?"

"Get into a strong stance." He demonstrated by standing a little taller and squaring his shoulders. "Steel your mind. Be bold. Then, when you drill down into your power, be the alpha. Bend its will and demand its fealty."

Sure. Nothing like showing a non-entity inside of me who's boss.

I grumbled under my breath as I pulled my shoulders

back.

"Is that really the strongest stance you can take?"

"Don't distract me."

He used his grip on my hands to twist me around so that my back pressed against him. "A powerful state doesn't just come from here." He dropped my hands and pulled my shoulders back against his body. I sucked in a breath.

Pressing an open hand firmly against my ribcage, he spoke into my ear. "Strength begins here."

My body reacted. I arched into him a little before I realized what I was doing.

He sucked in a breath, and his fingers tightened.

I jerked away from him and whirled around, assuming a fighting stance.

Kai nodded. "Better."

I bared my teeth at him.

"Now, drill into your power with that same dominance."

I was loath to obey anything he said, but if I could master this power, it would keep Lyric safer in the long run.

And in the short run, I'll be able to get out of this circle and away from Kai.

Mentally, I punched down into the red light and demanded the power submit to my will. The impression I got was that the power wasn't convinced I was really in charge.

I pushed.

It pushed back.

I gritted my teeth and threatened to never let it out again if it didn't cooperate.

It seemed to mock me.

This is ridiculous. I feel like I'm fighting with myself.

I clenched my fists as I concentrated. My nails dug into my palms.

The red power surged up through me, and I tried to wrestle it.

I ended up blasting Kai back against the barrier with a huge crimson orb. A crack splintered outward from where his head hit the dome.

He stood and brushed his pants off. "I didn't think you'd have quite that much kick left after the first round."

"Be careful. I might not be so gentle next time." I was bluffing, but hoped he wouldn't realize I'd lost the inner battle.

The dragonborn smiled.

I think I just earned a little predator respect.

"You have no control."

Or not.

"Try again."

You've got to be kidding.

A dozen failed attempts to wrestle my power into submission. A dozen times, Kai stood his ground against my attacks. He had to have increased his strength somehow because I was hitting hard every time.

Out of breath, my muscles shaking, I wanted to be done. Though I could keep pulling magic from the earth, my body was not used to this kind of a workout.

The more he stood there, pushing me to try again and do it better, the more I wanted to put him on the ground with his superior attitude. It was getting old.

"I'm done."

He shook his head. "You're done when I say you're done."

I stepped forward, balling my hands into fists. "You have no right to treat people like this."

He raised his eyebrows, challenge in his eyes. "Again."

"No." My tone was icy and calm. "I said I'm done."

I matched his hard look.

We held eye contact.

Finally, he growled and then bent down to pick up one of the discs at the edge of the circle. The barrier vanished. I left him there and headed back to camp.

TEN

"Woah, what happened to your clothes?" Tyler asked when I walked into camp in just Kai's t-shirt.

"I burnt them."

"What—"

"Don't ask." I continued to stalk past Tyler, ordering him to keep watch so that I could take some time alone at the stream.

Noticing a few of the same long purple and white thorny plants that had wounded Gemma's mother, I was careful to keep my distance.

I washed my hands and face in the stream. It was so refreshing I waded in. Fuming over the training session and all the emotions it had triggered in me, I scrubbed the sweat and dust from my face and arms.

I refuse to cry. I will not lose focus. I will find Lyric and then get back to my life.

I could figure out how to control my magic without Kai and his hostile idea of help. I flopped down on the bank, letting my feet float in the current. Feeling more collected, I relaxed for a while, breathing in the peace of the scene around me.

The sun began setting and the colors—so vivid they looked photoshopped—inspired an urge to paint the scene. It soothed my soul as I drank in every detail, planning to recall it later when I had my palette and brushes.

I wondered if my KC Art Institute acceptance or rejection letter was sitting in the mailbox at home.

I hope I got in.

I hope we get home in time for me to enroll in classes before the ones I want are full.

I mentally calculated what the date was and realized that rent was two days past due. A pit formed in my stomach. How strange it was to be sitting here, thinking about these worries, so far from home.

Nothing I can do about it here. One problem at a time.

Focus on getting to Lyric.

I felt a sting on my calf and jerked my legs up out of the water. A thick green and yellow snake floated, coiled to strike a second time. I scrambled back. My sleeve caught on a small crop of thorns that had been hidden in other brush.

I grabbed a nearby rock and threw it. The snake slithered away. Heart hammering, I looked down at my leg. Blood trickled from two tiny punctures on my calf. I checked my torn sleeve. There was no blood.

Oh, my god.

I eyed the purple and white thorns, aware of how close I'd come to being poisoned.

I hurried back to camp. Wary of danger in every direction.

. . .

When I reached camp, Tyler was chatting at Kai, who was skinning some kind of small animal, and, thankfully, had another shirt on.

Tyler took one look at my face and stood. "Are you okay?"

Then Kai's head whipped up, too, a scowl on his face.

I nodded. "I... I think so." I walked over and presented my leg. "I got bit by a snake."

"Oh, no!" Tyler came around the fire for a closer look.

"What were you thinking? Going off alone?" Kai sounded even more grumpy than usual, and I was not in the mood to put up with him.

"Why are you an asshole?"

Kai growled.

I held his stare, defiant.

After a moment, he cocked his eyebrow and set down his kill. "Did you see what the snake looked like?"

"Bright green. Irregular yellow spots. Round head."

Kai nodded. "Good."

My anxiety eased. "Not poisonous?"

"Slightly poisonous."

"What?!" Tyler said.

"How is that good?" I threw up my hands.

"The effects will be minor. Dizziness. Vomit. Headache."

Familiar adversaries. Still, it really sucked.

Kai moved closer to me, then knelt to look at my calf. He poured water from his flask to rinse the blood from my leg, revealing the bite.

"Hold still." His large hand wrapped around my ankle. I bristled, but my stomach flipped.

What is wrong with me?

"I need to remove the venom." When he bent his head down, placing his mouth on my leg to suck the venom out, my face heated. Self-conscious about the situation and angry at my body's reaction to it.

Ugh. The sooner we can ditch this guy, the better.

"Oh, that's so cool!" Tyler said. "I've seen this in movies. I always wondered if it actually worked."

I thought about asking Tyler to swap places with Kai, but my gag reflex instantly informed me I didn't want that either.

Kai turned and spat the contents on the ground, then went back a second time.

I focused intently on the flames of the campfire.

Once Kai finished, he wiped his mouth and swished with water from his flask. He took supplies out of the pack Tyler had hauled all day. After applying some kind of salve from a tin box on the bite, he wrapped the wound with a long strip of cloth.

I grumbled a begrudging thanks in the dragonborn's general direction, then rummaged through the pack to find something to wear on my lower half. I found a pair of pants and shoved my legs into them. They were too big, but I was just glad to be fully clothed.

After a very gamey dinner—Kai was clearly not a chef, but we didn't starve—we all laid down and tried to sleep. I couldn't tell if I was feverish or if it was just cold, but between that and the hard ground, I didn't sleep well. Horrible dreams plagued me, and I shivered in the chill.

I jolted awake. It was still dark. Someone had given me a thin blanket, far too small to cover all of me. I fell back into a nightmare.

I woke again, crying out. Voices were close. They made little sense.

"Drenched in sweat..."

"Got the poison out..."

"Sick..."

"Not the symptoms..."

Something wet and bitter poured into my mouth. I coughed and sputtered, flailing my arms in panic.

My throat burned.

"Astrid, it's okay." Tyler held my head in his lap. "It's medicine. It should help you feel better."

The medicine seemed to clear my head a bit. I could understand more of what Tyler and Kai were saying.

Relieved to have a bearing, I clung to the arm beside my head. "Tyler, it was horrible!" I started to cry. "I dreamed they were burning my arm off, and Lyric was stuck in a painting."

Tyler gasped. "Oh my gosh, I had the exact same dream!"

My mind jolted from its hysteria. "You did?"

"Are you insane? Of course I didn't." Tyler smiled and shrugged. "Sorry, I know... It's not funny."

I laughed. It felt strange. Then I couldn't help but laugh some more.

"Okay, something's really wrong with her," Tyler said to Kai.

That made me laugh more, which turned into sobs, which turned into me rolling to the side and puking all over the blanket that had been laid over me.

"What is that on the back of her arm?" Kai's tone sounded sharp.

"Um, it looks like..."

My face hovered inches from my own vomit while they discussed the state of my flaming arm.

Kai growled. He did that a lot.

Tyler spoke. "I've seen little black veins like that before. Gemma's mom..."

"She's been scratched by an Ice Thorn." Kai's words sounded bleak.

"This is bad! What do we do?"

"The elixir I gave her slows the effects of most poisons, but the little she swallowed, she didn't keep down."

"Give her more."

"It won't be enough."

Hands hauled me over, and they poured more bitter liquid into my mouth. My jaw was forced shut. "Swallow it," Kai ordered.

I swallowed, and it burned the whole way down. I closed my eyes, willing myself to not puke again.

"She needs water from a fae stream," Kai said.

"Where do we find that?"

"Almost 300 kilometers in the wrong direction."

"That's like... days of walking!" Tyler hissed. "Gemma's mom was gone in like minutes."

I'm about to die. Who will protect...

"Lyric." I choked on the word.

"It's okay, Astrid," Tyler said. "Lyric's fine."

"It looks like the thorn barely broke her skin," Kai said. "With how far the poison has spread, and her ingesting a small amount of elixir, Astrid might survive until daybreak."

"How fast could you fly there and bring the water back to her?"

"Even at my highest speed, which I couldn't sustain that entire distance, she would be gone long before I returned."

"There has to be something we can do."

I didn't hear Kai's response. I didn't hear anything else. I fell into another fitful sleep of nightmares.

I woke on the floor of a dark forest. There was no campfire, but the chill of the night was no longer plaguing my body. The glow of the moons coming through the trees reflected off the bare chest of the dragonborn sitting next to me. His eyes watched for something in the distance.

I jolted to a sitting position. "Where are we?"

"Good. You're feeling better. Be quiet." He continued to study the tree line.

"Why are you always rude?" I hissed. "And why don't you have a shirt on?"

"You didn't seem to mind it on the flight over."

"What?"

"Don't worry. I rejected your advances, and you went back to your old, bitter, angry self."

That can't be true.

I felt my face heat.

And he's the one with the personality problem.

"Just... put your shirt on."

His shoulders heaved a weary breath as he turned his face towards me. "I only brought one spare, and you vomited on it. There wasn't time to wash it before we left."

I looked down at my shirt—Kai's shirt.

At least one of us is wearing it.

When I looked up, I noticed him wince, though it looked like he'd tried to hide it. He was holding his left bicep.

"What happened to your arm?"

His eyes scanned the edge of the forest again. "A nine-hour flight without rest—even someone your size becomes considerably difficult to carry."

"I thought you didn't carry people."

He made that rumbling noise.

I reached around and felt my arm. It didn't feel like it was on fire anymore.

"So, did we get the healing water, or whatever?"

"If we hadn't, you would be dead." Kai didn't bother to look at me.

"How long was I out?"

"You finally slept without thrashing after you drank the fae water. I'd say that was maybe five or six hours ago."

"So we lost like fifteen hours, and we're still nine hours off track?"

"It'll take us longer to get back to your friend."

"Why?"

"Safer to slow down. And you'll probably need to stop a few times."

"Let's get going then." I stood brushing off my oversized pants.

Kai turned, and his eyes glinted. "We are in the heart of

fae territory. We'll lay low until daybreak." He turned his attention back to the trees. "Get some rest."

I sat back down.

Realizing that Kai had just put a solid amount of effort into saving my life, and was clearly exhausted, I offered to keep watch while he rested—though it pained me a little to do it.

When he refused, I took offense.

Does he think I'm incapable?

I told him, in no uncertain terms, that I wouldn't take no for an answer. I also begrudgingly promised to wake him at the first sign of trouble.

The dragonborn finally relented and laid down. I watched him out of the corner of my eye as he adjusted to get comfortable. He closed his eyes, and I studied his sharp, handsome features.

I'm alive because this man saved me.

And he probably thought I was ungrateful.

I looked away from him when I spoke. "You're not as evil as people think you are."

"I'm worse."

I rolled my eyes. "Well, thanks for saving my life."

"I'm being well paid."

Ah. There it is... at least he's honest.

I wrapped my arms tight around my knees.

I guess that's what I get for trying to be nice to an assassin.

I didn't know how long Kai had been asleep, but I had to pee. He had implied that this forest was dangerous, but I wouldn't go far. I tiptoed far enough away to feel like I could take care of it. The walk back seemed to take longer than I remembered. Had I gotten turned around?

I backtracked, retracing my steps again, and soon nothing looked familiar. I was far too close to the edge of the trees. The clearing nearby was bright with moonlight. There was a beautiful brook with a gentle waterfall. Flowers peppered the land and music reached my ears, inviting me to step into the moonlight and bask in the serenity.

I made my way to the clearing, a place so lovely and safe, I didn't understand why this hadn't been our destination all along.

Everything in my life was leading me to this place. Of course we should have come here. Why had we been trying to go anywhere else?

On the edge of the stream was a huge, enchanting tree with twisting white bark and big leaves that shone in the moonlight.

Staring at the tree, which seemed to breathe life into every part of the universe, I plopped myself down in the plush grass and heaved a tremendous sigh of relief. All of my burdens had just evaporated. I drank it in with a lazy smile.

My arm was suddenly and brutally yanked up by my dark, loathsome companion.

"Ow!" My voice came out lazy and petulant. "Why do you have to be so miserable?" I pulled against his hold. "I'm tired. I want to rest here in this beautiful place and look at this beautiful tree."

"Astrid." Kai held me and whispered in my ear in a way that was not romantic despite us being in the most romantic place of all time. "This place is not beautiful." His tone was warning, and his grip on my arm was bruising.

"Just because you're too negative, and violent, and disgusting, and..."

"Snap out of it." He growled.

I gave him a cruel smile. "You're not even human. Of course, you don't appreciate this place. You're just a dragonborn. An animal."

Kai's expression cracked for just a moment before his scowl returned. I felt triumphant having wounded him.

He turned me to face him square on. "Astrid, listen to me." He shook my shoulders. "It's a trick."

"You're hurting me. Let me go!" I pushed against his chest. He held me tighter and pulled me closer. Sweat beaded on his skin, and he looked around hopelessly, searching for something.

An emotion like desperation flashed in his eyes. He growled and dipped his head down, placing his open mouth to my sneering lips. My heart stopped. Kai breathed warm air into me, filling up my lungs.

His mouth was insistent on mine, and my lips softened and opened against his. My body melted as his hands traveled up my arms and tangled in my hair, cradling my head. His tongue teased mine.

My head was suddenly unclouded, everything in sharp focus even as everything in me reacted to his touch. My hands found the warm skin of his back. I pulled him in, desperate for the space between us to disappear.

He gently tugged my bottom lip between his teeth as he pulled away.

I looked into his eyes and gasped. It was like I'd never seen him clearly before. He was beautiful. Even more than I'd realized before. More than any man I'd ever seen. The piercing gray of his human eyes seemed to come from the semi-transparent overlay of dragon's eyes. Out of his dark hair, loomed three gently curving horns on each side of his head. Each horn pointed towards the back, in succession down his head. And the two bottom horns, near his ears, extended into his cheekbones, giving him an almost elven look. A virile warrior, even a god, amidst mortal creatures.

Kai's wings towered above us, half folded. Before, I'd thought they were dark and terrifying, but now I realized that they were captivating. A piece of dramatic artwork. Vast in size and translucent black in color, with solid black markings that mirrored the tribal tattoos adorning his bicep, pec, and shoulder.

Fascinated, I reached up to brush my fingers along the protrusion on his cheek. "What did you do to me?" I whispered, breathless.

Kai slowly turned me around to see the clearing and what I saw filled me with fear and horror.

No longer was the clearing filled with music, and peace, and beauty. The entire place had become a swamp. Mist hung in the air like a warning for anyone smart enough to heed it. The water in the stream and coming down the waterfall ran thick and black as pitch. The tree that had looked so beautiful before was now bare and haunting as a skeleton with mossy vines hanging from its branches. I pressed my back into Kai's chest, trying to distance myself from the horror I was facing.

Here and there, little red eyes were watching us. Their owners seemed to hum some kind of dissonant and terrifying melody.

"What happened to the clearing?"

Kai whispered, keeping us both very still. "I breathed dragon sight into you. Until it wears off, you can see through any glamour."

"That was all—"

"An illusion. Meant to lure and entrap anyone foolish enough to come this close."

"What are all those creatures watching us?" The eyes were inching closer and closer.

"They're fae sprites." He pulled me back a little. "They really like your kind. It's why I had you hidden far into the forest."

Fear gripped me.

The sprites grew more bold, and a few began rushing at us.

Kai growled. A now familiar sound, that in this moment felt comforting. His arms snaked around my middle. We shot up into the air. Wind rushed past me, along with leaves and branches.

We were above the trees. Several winged sprites flying after us.

"Be quiet!" Kai snapped.

I hadn't realized I was screaming. I bit my lip to keep quiet, clutching his arms, as we flew higher and higher.

"Breathe, Astrid."

I sucked in air, not realizing I'd been holding my breath.

We raced higher with each pump of the Dragonborn's wings. He banked and his wings folded, shooting us into an angled dive. My stomach dropped.

"Oh my god, please don't drop me."

"Don't tempt me." He tilted his chin.

I clutched at his arms. "Don't you dare!"

"I didn't before."

I caught a glimpse of the beady red eyes that were in pursuit. "Are they going to catch us?"

"I can't outrun them for long with you weighing me down."

"That is *not* very comforting."

We climbed again, higher and higher, breaking through the clouds and then changing directions.

"If we can't outrun them, what are we gonna do?"

Kai glanced behind us. "When we cross out of fae territory, they won't follow."

"Why the heck were we camping out there then?"

He growled. "You were dying, and I needed a fucking break."

The sprites were just yards behind us. Kai's chest rumbled with another growl. It reverberated through my whole body.

We aren't going to make it.

I closed my eyes, telling myself that I wasn't flying through the air and about to fall to my death.

My red magic flashed, eager to be let out. I didn't want to end up naked again, but I also didn't want to end up dead.

Sprites began latching onto my legs. I kicked frantically. Kai held me tight, but the sprites were ripping me away. I was hanging by just my arms, sweat on my skin making me slip away even more.

I screamed and unleashed red light. Four sprites fell in a blaze. I triumphantly noted that I didn't lose my clothes this time.

Kai let me go, and I fell. My stomach lurched so that I couldn't even scream.

His wings folded and he dove. I plummeted for much longer than was necessary before he caught me around the waist. Then I wrapped my legs and arms around him, holding on with all my strength.

After that, I kept my eyes closed as we flew.

Finally, we landed.

"Let go," Kai said, shaking me off.

I peeked an eye open. We were on a rocky hill, surrounded by more forest. I set my trembling legs down and then shoved his chest. "You asshole! You dropped me!"

"I caught you." He rolled his shoulder.

I sat down, shaking from a concoction of fear, adrenaline, and using my magic ungrounded.

"You said you wouldn't drop me."

"Relax." He walked away.

I looked behind me. "What if more of those red-eyed Gollum things come?"

"They won't. We're out of fae territory." He sounded so unconcerned it was irritating.

He began collecting wood. "We'll camp here and head back in the morning."

My gaze kept darting around, and I backed up to be a little closer to the dragonborn with his wings and his horns, an apex predator.

Once the fire was lit, he ordered me to sleep.

Like it would be easy to drift off after almost dying. My muscles quivered as I moved to lay near the fire.

"Your body wasn't fully healed." He glanced over at me,

his horns glinting in the light of the fire. "You shouldn't have used your magic."

"Well, someone had to save us." I wrapped my trembling arms around myself.

"You still have no control." He shook his head.

I glared at him. "I didn't even burn my clothes this time."

"That's because you're wearing my clothes, which are fireproof." He looked at me with a pointed expression.

Dang...

Kai unstrapped his weapons and made a pillow for himself out of the handle of his large ax. Though I would never tell him so, I was relieved when he laid down next to me rather than across the fire. I didn't think I would have been able to close my eyes with my back exposed to the night and whatever lurked out there.

Eventually my breathing calmed, and my body warmed enough to relax. As I lay there, watching the embers dance with light, I was very aware of the solid presence of the dragonborn close behind me. I brought my fingers to gently brush my lips where Kai had kissed me. I took a shuddering breath and drew my bottom lip between my teeth.

Holy crap...

ELEVEN

I woke in the morning to Kai's boot prodding my shoulder. "Get up."

My brain kicked into fight or flight. I sat up so fast my vision blacked. "Did they follow us?"

"No. Just ready to head out." His tone was spartan, and it grated my jittery nerves. The sun hadn't even risen yet.

I rubbed the sleep from my eyes. "Why the sudden rush?"

"A contract just came in, so I want to get this job back on track and be done with you and your friend."

I scowled in his direction. "Something we can agree on." The dragon sight had worn off. He looked human again. Still, his words felt like a slap in the face after the events of the night before.

You knew he was a dick, Astrid. Him kissing you doesn't change that.

No matter how mind blowing that kiss was.

I seriously regretted my hormones driving that moment.

Not how I'd imagined my first kiss happening.

I'd planned on it being sweet and romantic with someone who really cared about me.

Not an assassin who'd callously drop me near death as soon as it was over.

I hauled my sore body up. I took my hair down from its disheveled braid and re-did the plait.

When I get back to earth, I am going to take the longest shower of my life.

Kai was scattering the remnants of the fire, and I noticed he still seemed to favor his left arm.

Since he was carrying me back, I didn't like the idea of him having an injury.

"Hey, do you want me to use some of my healing magic on that?"

How hard can it be?

"No."

"It's way more cooperative than the red." I tried to sound confident. I was dying to test my orange magic, and I also didn't want him to drop me on the flight back.

"I'm fine." He rolled his shoulder. "And I don't trust you."

"Well, maybe I don't trust you." I folded my arms. "If you're going to fly me back, I want you to be able to handle it."

"I can handle it."

I looked at his powerful, injured arm pointedly.

"All I have to do is fly." Kai gestured for me to come to him. "You'll be the one holding yourself up now that you're coherent."

"Fine." I stepped up to face him. "How long did you say this flight is?"

"It was nine hours the first time. But I doubt you'll be able to handle that without stopping." He adjusted his weapons belt. His shirtless bronze torso mocked my ability to focus.

This is going to be a long flight.

"How did you even fly that?" I hoped conversation would distract me.

"I'm dragonborn."

Apparently that explains all the things.

Kai used the weapons belt to help secure me to him.

Straddling someone that I found attractive but irritating, for such a long time, was maybe the most awkward thing I've ever done.

My traitorous body felt differently than I did about the whole thing. I was a lot warmer in places I didn't want to think about. It helped to remind myself that he could drop me again at any moment.

But sometimes, my mind would helpfully volunteer to replay the kiss from the night before.

Then my self-talk came in strong.

A one-time thing. Won't happen again.

Focus on Lyric and art school.

He's an assassin from another realm, Astrid. A seriously bad person. I'm not in the market for any guy, let alone one like that.

Aside from the inner dialogue, there wasn't much conversation. There was an unspoken temporary truce between us while we were in the air.

Looking at the ground far below made me nauseous. I

was glad when we'd fly above the clouds and I could imagine that they were a giant pillow that would support me if I fell.

I passed a lot of time studying Kai's wings. They didn't look leathery and terrifying like they had the first couple of times I'd seen them. Though I couldn't see Kai's horns, his wings still looked as they had when I'd had dragon sight. Glass-like black, with dark markings that mirrored his tribal tattoos.

Now I noticed that there were places where dark, jagged scars interrupted the symmetrical designs in the fleshy parts of the wings.

Like bat wings, each had four bone-tipped peaks along the base, and one large dark claw at the single crest on top.

The wings faded into the dragonborn's back in a shadowy, nebulous way. Contrary to what I'd first imagined, it was not like Wolverine's claws, where they shot out of his body when he needed them. It actually seemed to be more of a phantom-wings-appear-when-he-wants-them kind of thing.

Mile after mile, they beat a steady rhythm. When he stretched them out to full capacity, the flesh between each base-tip rippled a little in the wind as we skimmed through the air.

"How come your wings look like this sometimes, but sometimes look... different?"

I didn't say scary, because I was trying to maintain that fragile truce while we were stuck together.

"Because I'm not using my glamour." He stared straight ahead.

"But I can't see your horns."

He glanced at me and then away. "Well, I'm using a little.

Trying to spare you where I can." I was so close that I noticed the subtle movement when he clenched his jaw.

That's uncharacteristically thoughtful. Though I really didn't mind the way he'd looked without glamour.

"But it requires too much energy to glamour my wings and fly this far with a burden."

Oh, there's the dig.

And I was about to tell him I thought his horns were actually pretty cool.

He could go ahead and expend extra energy on glamour.

I didn't complain about his word choice to him. Again with the truce I'd pledged to myself. I didn't want to give him a reason to loosen that belt and let me fall to my death.

The flight was long. We stopped a few times for things like food and water. Mostly we stopped because even being strapped to him, my arms and legs were struggling to keep me up. My muscles burned.

Kai seemed to sense when my grip was about to give out. Several times, he wrapped his powerful arms around me and allowed me to relax into his support for a while. Maybe the kindest gesture he'd ever made.

'I'm being well paid.' His words echoed in my head, a reminder that with him, it wasn't genuine kindness.

In the afternoon, we stopped for a bit in a meadow with a vast river flowing through. My lips parted as I took in the view. The field was full of wild flowers in hues ranging all over the palette. It was breathtaking and went for miles. I turned in a slow circle trying to memorize every detail. My eyes landed on the dragonborn who was filling his water flask from a river. I noticed that his hair was all shoulder length where I thought there had been one part that was a long Viking braid before.

"Did you cut your hair?"

He glanced back at me but said nothing.

I tilted my head and narrowed my eyes. "Didn't you used to have a long warrior braid?"

"I traded it." He kept his eyes on the flask he was filling.

"For what?"

"The fae don't give anything for free. Not even their water."

"Oh." My voice came out small.

He took a long pull from his flask. A heaviness hung in the air around me. I didn't know what his braid had meant to him, or what it had cost him to trade it away, and I couldn't bring myself to ask.

He must really want my mother's cuff. How valuable is that stone I've worn on my arm my whole life, for him to go to all this trouble?

Though I knew Kai had saved me because he was being paid, my life was important to me—and I was grateful.

"Thank you, for getting me the fae water."

He nodded once. "Let's go."

The rest of the journey was awkward and quiet, and I found myself looking forward to Tyler's chattiness.

. . .

After an endless day of flying, we descended near the camp where we'd left Tyler. It was late in the evening, and the sun was setting.

Two days officially wasted.

We landed in the clearing where we had done training. My arms and legs were shaky from holding myself up most of the day. When Kai set me down and untethered us, I wobbled.

Kai drew his ax, and I scowled. "What are you doing?"

"Shh." He put a finger to his lips. "Someone's close."

"It's probably Tyler."

I hope it's just Tyler.

"Not Tyler's scent." Kai's nostrils flared. "It's a dragon."

I froze. "Are dragons bad?"

He threw me a sideways glance. "Dragons are just like any other species. They come in all varieties."

My chest tightened and my fingers reached for Mom's cuff to find comfort in the stone that was no longer there. I followed Kai as he crept alongside the hill that hid our camp from view.

Tyler's voice floated in from around the bend. "Sometimes I still play D&D with my old buddies, but since I moved, it's all online now. Anyway, since I met Lyric, Kansas City has actually been pretty great."

"Clearly, whoever he's talking to isn't a threat." I stalked around Kai. He grabbed my arm to pull me back, a warning in his expression.

I rolled my eyes at him and gestured for him to lead the way with his battle ax.

When we rounded the boulder that hid the campsite, I saw Tyler stroking the oversized head of a brown dragon.

I wasn't sure how big dragons usually were, but this one was about the size of a horse.

The dragon lifted its head and bared its teeth, emitting a growl. I froze. Its green eyes locked on us. Beside me, Kai also growled.

"It's okay, buddy." Tyler scrambled to his feet. "These are the friends I was telling you about who are helping me find Lyric."

The dragon swiveled its head. Kai stared it down for a beat before lowering his weapon. The assassin held out his fist to the dragon, inclining his head slightly. The dragon, inclined its head then came forward to touch its nose to Kai's outstretched fist.

"See, buddy?" Tyler stroked the dragon's neck. "They're okay."

My mouth hung open slightly. "You made friends with a dragon?"

This is unreal.

"He was stuck in some kind of rusty trap down the hill." Tyler indicated the direction. "I got him out and bandaged up his wing." He scratched under the dragon's chin. "We've been chilling here all day while he rests, haven't we, buddy?"

"Her name is Sakashi." Kai jerked his chin towards her.

"Oh!" Tyler said. "Sakashi! That's cool. Do you know her?"

Kai shook his head. "Dragonborn can communicate with all dragon species."

"Like telepathically?" I asked.

Kai nodded. "Sakashi here is a young wyvern." He gestured towards her feet. "Two legs instead of four."

"She's... amazing," I breathed.

"Isn't she?" Tyler continued to pet her. "It's like the coolest thing that's ever happened to me! Lyric is going to flip when she hears how I rescued a dragon. I'll never be able to go back to normal life after spending the day with a dragon."

I smiled. "I can't wait to go back to normal life." I eyed the dragon's long barbed tail and burnt umber scales flecked with metallic gold. "But I am definitely going to paint a picture of her."

"Do you know if she understands what I'm saying when I talk to her?" Tyler asked Kai. "She kinda seems to like when I talk to her."

Kai nodded. "Dragons can understand all languages, but they only speak to others through the mind."

"So, why doesn't she speak to me?" Tyler ran a hand in his red hair.

"She's young." Kai shrugged. "She's still learning. There's an art to speaking into a non-dragon mind, and each mind is a little different."

"Is there a way to help? I'd really like to understand her."

"If you had temporary dragon sight, you and she could forge a path into your mind." Kai folded his bronze arms thoughtfully. "Once she has a pathway, you'd be able to communicate with her freely after that."

"Awesome! How can I get some dragon sight?"

I turned away, thinking of the heated kiss that had given me temporary dragon sight.

"Tyler, I don't think you're going to want to—"

"Woah, this is so cool!" Tyler said. "Dude, you have epic horns!"

"Thanks," Kai said.

I whirled around to find that Kai, from two yards away, had given Tyler dragon sight.

My mouth hung open as I watched Tyler bask in his new clarity.

When Tyler turned to talk to the wyvern, I folded my arms and looked at Kai, my eyebrows raised. "No mouth to mouth?"

He shrugged and turned away. "Unnecessary." I caught a glimpse of his suppressed smile.

I stepped around him so he had to look at me. My voice lowered to a whisper. "So, what was that little stunt in the fae land?"

Another shrug. "A little payback for you being such a pain in my ass."

"You ba—"

"You enjoyed it."

I gasped and recoiled. "How dare you!"

He spread his arms with a cocky expression. "Not my fault you're easy to rile."

"You are despicable."

"You have no idea." He leaned in, his face hardening. "It would fill your sheltered little mind with horror if you knew the things I've done."

He stepped around me, leaving me with no comeback as he approached the wyvern.

Shake it off, Astrid. You knew he was a bad guy. Let's just see this mission through and get home.

I squared my shoulders. Maybe I was sheltered. But I

vowed I would not be so 'easy to rile' from here on out.

Reining in my emotions, and putting my thoughts in check, I turned to find Tyler, Kai, and the young dragon having a silent exchange.

Kai stepped over to examine the injured wing. Tyler followed, and I tagged along. Sakashi's large head swiveled to watch us.

"How bad is it?" Tyler looked at Kai.

"It's bad."

"Will she be able to fly again?" I asked. Proud of myself for how totally calm and collected I came across.

"That's what Sakashi is worried about," Tyler said. "A dragon who can't fly is disavowed by its kind."

"That's terrible."

"Tyler did a good job of splinting the break, but a wing is complex, and their injuries are dangerous." The dragonborn stepped back a little. "If it doesn't heal right, she'll wish she had found death."

I thought about the scars on Kai's wings.

"Is it the same for a dragonborn?" I asked. Imagining the assassin in battle, protecting his wings at all costs.

"It's a little different," Kai said. "But yes, a dragonborn's wings are vital."

"Will you ask her if she'll let me use orange light magic to help her?"

"Your instincts to ask permission are wise." There was no mistaking Kai's expression. My judgment had impressed him. I felt smug about it.

After he and Sakashi had a silent conversation, he nodded at me. "She'll allow it."

Kai cleared his throat and stepped away.

I let my toes work the dust in the rocky ground until I found a comfortable stance. Taking a deep, calming breath, I let my eyes fall closed.

A smile touched my lips when I found the playful orange light in my core. It felt intuitive to work with it. I imagined bringing it out into a translucent orb, as I'd seen Khandra do. I opened my eyes, and the light flowed through my hands and manifest into a perfect melon-size sphere.

Now that the magic hovered between my hands, I wished I'd asked Khandra more questions.

I decided to just feign confidence and press forward. Focusing my thoughts on one simple directive: "Make this wing perfect."

I mentally repeated the command over and over with the orb floating in my palms, then continued the mantra as I pressed the magic into the injured wing. The solidity of the magic surprised me when I began pushing it into the wyvern. Like pushing a balloon under water. I redoubled my focus on the directive and used both hands to guide the light into the bloodstained, broken wing.

Finally, orange light coalesced with the site. The scales around the injury flashed with a glow before fading to their mottled brown color.

I let my arms drop to my sides, feeling even more exhausted than I had when I'd used my red light magic. Even with being grounded.

We all watched as the wound began to slowly fade from view.

"I did it." It came out in a whisper.

"Wow, Astrid," Tyler was smiling at me, wonder in his expression.

I grinned at Tyler. Then looked over at Kai, who looked away quickly.

The dragonborn cleared his throat and stalked away, a scowl on his face.

I sat down, wanting to rest, but not taking my eyes off the healing process. It was thrilling to watch, knowing that I had created such a miracle.

This is going to change Lyric's life. Never again will she have a wheelchair day.

TWELVE

I could see why Tyler enjoyed hanging out with the wyvern. It was calming to be near her.

While she healed, she slept. I watched the rise and fall of the dragon's body as she breathed. Her scales rippled and moved—each a separate piece of intricate armor that fit together. It was almost as fascinating to watch as the steady healing of her wing.

When the light faded from the sky, we all slept. The assassin on one side of the campfire, me and Tyler on the other, the ground beneath me a supporting ally, and the wyvern curled up at our feet. I felt, for the first time in a long time, like I wasn't exposed. My body relaxed into the sensation, and my sleep was peaceful.

The following morning, a large gust of wind woke me. The wyvern was testing her massive wings, both of which were whole. After a few flaps, she took off in flight. She let out a triumphant cry as she circled the camp overhead.

"There she goes!" Tyler said. "Well done, Astrid!"

"Even with healing magic, I've never seen a wing that badly damaged fly again." Kai kept his eyes on the sky.

"Careful," I said. "That almost sounded like praise."

The wyvern circled higher, her form shrinking into the distance.

I craned my neck, watching her leave. "She's not coming back, is she?"

"She's off to find her family," Tyler said. "But she promised to find me again someday."

"That might be hard when we're back home."

Tyler shrugged. "I saved a freaking dragon. Anything's possible."

We gathered our things. After the long detour, I was anxious to get our journey back on track.

To Death's Gate. Find Lyric. Get home. I didn't think I would ever need another adventure after this.

Crossing the sparse, rocky, mountain ridge into the valley below took an entire day.

When we arrived at what Kai said was Death's Gate, it wasn't what I'd imagined. The 'gate' was two mountainous rocks crashed together at the tops, forming a crude triangular opening.

Clearly we had been traveling on the 'hell' side of the gate; because, in contrast to the sparse, dry, rocky terrain we had just traversed, the scene through the gate sprawled a lush, inviting woodland.

"How is this kind of transition even possible?" I asked.

"Once we pass this gate, we enter the territory of the Suv

race," Kai said. "Many of them wield blue light magic, so their land is rich in water."

"What was the place we just traveled through?" Tyler asked.

"The North Wilds. No one lives there."

Partway into the forest, we made camp for another night under a giant moss-covered tree.

One more night. Then we find Lyric and head home. I smiled at the thought of sleeping in my own bed and being able to sit and paint in the calm serenity of our simple apartment.

In the morning, we continued south, eventually finding the well from Ro's directions. Deep green vines clung to the sides of the well. The foliage was so thick, I would have missed it. Kai spotted it because, apparently, the foliage was mostly an illusion made of magic to hide the landmark, making it a poor disguise for someone with dragon sight.

From the well, we headed east, following what Kai was certain was a path. I was banking on the assumption that he knew what he was talking about.

Once the path forked, I could see that he was right. We followed the left fork, eventually finding a stream, as promised.

With every new direction, I felt encouraged that Ro had given good directions, and I was relieved I had remembered them.

Following the water upstream, we finally heard crashing water. My heart soared, knowing that the journey was coming to an end. I couldn't see much of the sky, but what I could see told me it was getting late in the day. The terrain was complex but not difficult to navigate. The waterfall proved very secluded. I doubted many people would have stumbled upon the location without specific directions.

We skirted the waterfall single file. Kai led the way. I followed, with Tyler on my heels. Though we were a safe distance behind the raining water, spray tickled my face.

Before I rounded the final bend of the rock, I heard Kai's familiar growl.

When I caught up to him, I was greeted with the long end of a weapon in my face. The man wielding it was possibly even shorter than I was, with an unkempt beard. My hands came up in surrender. A taller guard, with dark skin, had his weapon trained on Kai. The dragonborn made an irritated sound and reluctantly brought his hands up as well.

Tyler, in the middle of saying how cool this whole place was, stopped short.

"Oh, my bad." He brought his hands up too.

I explained to the men that we were friends. "Just here to meet up with my sister before we turn right around to leave."

The tall one kept his eyes fixed on Kai as he spoke. "This soldier is no friend of ours."

"He's not a soldier. He's with us." I insisted.

"All dragonborn are military." The guard's expression was full of disgust. "Alifar practically owns the bloodline."

Another low growl from Kai told me he wasn't a fan of this conversation.

Would he turn assassin on these guys and get us kicked out before we even got in the door? Not if I have anything to say about it. I stepped in front of Kai, my hands still raised. "We're only here to fetch my sister. What can we do to prove to you we're not your enemies?"

"Who's your sister?" The short guard asked.

I described her silver eyes—her most defining feature—and explained that she had come with Ro.

Judging from the glance the guards shared, that information seemed to help our case.

"Your sister has silver eyes?" the taller guard asked.

"Yeah. I know that sounds weird, but it's true."

"Ro sent you?" the shorter one asked.

"Yeah. He's the one who told us how to find this place."

The two men looked at each other before nodding in agreement.

"Okay, follow us," tall guy said. "You'll have to leave your weapons here."

Kai rolled his eyes and growled again, but began unstrapping his weapons and laying them in a neat pile at the side of the cave. The pile was not small.

I got the impression that Kai was posturing to show them that he didn't need weapons to take them both out.

The guards took us further into the cave, which boasted a single door. Short guy approached the door and put his hand on the edge. The door lit up just briefly before opening.

Stepping into their base we entered a long hallway with natural stone walls and floors, reminding me of the fact that we were, in fact, in a cave. What looked like florescent lights flickered above our heads.

"I didn't think you guys had electricity here," I said.

"It's not electricity. It's magic." Kai was glancing around, clearly assessing his surroundings with his ex-military perspective.

"Why haven't we seen these anywhere else?" Tyler pointed to the lights.

"Not everyone lives secluded in the forest, mostly relying on their own resources." Kai eyed at an overhead vent as we passed.

I realized he referred to Khandra.

"What about the village near the Jalak port?" Tyler asked.

"There's little magic on the outskirts," Kai said. "Jalak are bottom feeders."

"That's kind of harsh," the short, bearded guard said. His gray camo jacket label read Brewhood.

The tall guard shrugged. "Anyone who opposes the Brotherhood is a step closer to earning my respect."

"Not all Jalak are part of the brotherhood," Brewhood said.

"Might as well be," Kai scoffed.

After following the guards down a couple of hallways and past several large wooden doors, they ushered us into a small room and told us to wait. There was nothing in the space but two simple wooden chairs. The guards left, and when they shut the door, a strange emptiness gutted my insides. I sucked in a breath and felt the familiar aura of a migraine threatening.

"What happened?" Tyler asked.

"This room is equipped with a magic suppression spell." Kai stepped over to the door. I noticed his glamour had fallen away to reveal his wings and horns. In spite of myself, the view sent a thrill through my core.

"It's locked." He gave a quiet snort.

Panic rose in my chest. "Are they keeping us prisoner?"

"We're only in this room for as long as I allow it," Kai said, folding his arms and leaning against the wall. "Even without magic, I can tear my way out of this base the moment I choose."

"I guess it's good they don't know that," I said.

"Oh, they know. I'm dragonborn."

"Why would they put you in a room like this, then?" Tyler asked.

"Makes the by-blows feel safer."

Eventually, three rebels came in to talk to us. Kai took a slightly wider stance and unfolded his arms. One rebel was the short, bearded guard, Brewhood. Kai had informed us he was a halfling—part dwarf, part human. The next was a plump, balding gentleman with a goatee. He looked human. And the third was a woman about my age with a low, tight ponytail, pointed elf ears, and severe resting bitch face. The two men wore full black and gray camo. The woman wore a beige blouse and slacks.

The plump man introduced himself as August Neeman, vice commander of the rebel force. "I'm told you were sent by Ro. I want to know where you saw him last."

"Well, he should be here," I said. "He told me this is where he was bringing my sister."

"He's not here," the halfling said.

The commander nodded. "His comm went dark almost two weeks ago, and we haven't been able to make contact."

Blood drained from my head.

"What does that mean?" I glanced between the rebels. "I

was with him on a Jalak slave ship just a few days ago. His instructions to come here were very clear."

"Your sister is the one with silver eyes?" It was the elven woman who spoke.

Commander August gestured to the female. "This is Freya Cardalan. She's a historian, and an expert on the andeo race."

"What does that have to do with finding Ro or Lyric?"

The woman stepped towards me. "I heard about your sister and have some questions."

"Later, Freya," the halfling cut in. "If Ro really found an andeo, he probably needs backup. We need to figure out where he is."

"I agree." I gestured to the guard. "We need to find them."

"Would Ro betray you if he got his hands on something as valuable as an andeo?" All eyes turned to Kai.

I shook my head in confusion. "What is this andeo?"

"Ro is like a brother to me." The halfling puffed up his chest. "He would never sell out."

"Calm down, Hiram." The commander placed a meaty hand on the guard's shoulder. "No one is questioning Ro's loyalty."

"What is andeo?" I asked again.

"Your sister," Kai said.

"You think Lyric is a what now?" Tyler asked.

"Andeo," Freya said.

When we didn't appear properly impressed, she added, "The race of goddesses?"

"Goddess?" I couldn't wrap my head around it.

"No, that kind of makes sense," Tyler said, shrugging.

The rebels looked at us like we were idiots.

"They're from the Realm of Stars," Kai said. "They know nothing."

No, but Kai sure seemed to. Was that why he was helping us? To get his hands on Lyric because she was apparently valuable?

The commander turned to face me. "Are you telling me you didn't know what your sister was?"

"Well, how do you know what she is?" I said. "You haven't even met her."

"If she truly has silver eyes, like you say, there's no other explanation." Freya opened her palm and waved her other hand in a strange pattern, causing a holographic picture to appear. The woman in the snapshot had dark hair, dark skin, and silver eyes that mirrored Lyric's.

My mouth fell open slightly at the sight. This girl could have been Lyrics biological sister.

"Alifar hunts them down and sacrifices them."

My chest tightened at the revelation. That man would not get his hands on my sister.

She snapped her hand back, causing the picture to vanish. "It's how he's remained in power for almost two thousand years."

Lyric, where are you?

"If there's an R.O.S. andeo in this realm, then the plan we've worked on for over two generations is in danger." The commander's face was pale.

"What plan?" Tyler asked.

"We've been waiting for the High Lord's power to weaken enough that we have a fighting chance of overthrowing him," August said. "If Alifar gets his hands on an andeo..."

"He'll be as unbeatable as he's always been." Kai's horns made his expression more fierce. "You've never had a fighting chance, and that isn't going to change."

Clearly he has no love for these rebels. Did that mean that he really was loyal to Alifar? I'd gotten the impression in the spice shop that he despised the High Lord.

Could we trust him? He'd gotten us this far.

If he just wanted an andeo, he wouldn't have had to go to the trouble of saving my life.

The rebels discussed amongst themselves. I looked at Tyler and Kai, unsure of where to go from here.

Our mission hadn't changed. Find Lyric. Get home. This realm was more dangerous than I had even realized.

I heard one rebel say, "Kill her and eliminate the issue."

I whirled towards them. "What?"

Tyler looked as angry as I felt. Kai put a hand on his shoulder.

"If we take her power for ourselves, we level the playing field with the high lord," Freya said.

"Over my dead body," Tyler said.

"No one is killing my sister." I stared daggers at her.

Clearly she couldn't be trusted.

"No one should have that much power," Hiram said.

Another point the halfling and I agreed on.

. . .

"The only way to keep her out of Alifar's reach is to either kill her or force her ascension," Freya said, stepping forward.

This woman is evil.

If my magic weren't suppressed...

"We don't even know where Ro and the andeo are right now," August said, trying to placate both of us.

And I'm going to have to find Lyric first.

"Ro's probably lying low," Hiram said. "His family has a secure method to contact him when he goes undercover."

The vice commander nodded. "Yes. If we talk to them, they might know where he is, and we can provide reinforcements to keep the andeo out of Alifar's reach."

"Great, let's talk to his family." There, we had a direction to head in.

"They're in Sasca," Hiram said. "A city that's not even in this region."

"I'll send word to the outpost to inform Commander Dia," August said. "We can send a small recon team to Sasca in the morning."

"I'm going." I folded my arms.

The vice commander shook his head. "I'm not sending a stranger to where Ro's family lives."

"It's my sister. I'm going to be there when we find her."

"We can just take them to the edge of town and leave them to wait while we talk to his family," The halfling offered.

"No, I need to be there." I couldn't risk them finding her without me there to protect her.

"Waiting on the edge of Sasca is the best you're going to get," August said.

"Fine."

Tyler was quick to remind Kai that the agreement was to help until we found Lyric. If he left early, no payment would be given.

Kai grumbled something about it being a ridiculous and tedious job, but he still agreed to come. I trusted the dragonborn more than Freya at this point, so I was glad he was still on board.

The dwarf took us to a small room with two bunk beds to spend the night. I asked for clean clothes and a shower. They provided us access to the large community closet where we were each allotted one outfit. Kai just wanted his shirt back from me, and didn't accept the rebel's clothes. Tyler and I gave them our sizes, and I asked if they had anything fireproof. The closet attendant came back with a pair of black pants, dark green shirt and black combat jacket. He assured me they were fireproof and my size. At Kai's insistence, the attendant also handed me a pair of grounding shoes. They looked like regular black combat boots, but in each of the soles was a small, polished mineral that touched both the earth and the foot—allowing for an unbroken connection.

"Ditch the runners," Kai said, gesturing to my tennis shoes.

Once I scrubbed clean, I let the warm water of the shower pelt my back as I thought about all the unsettling information I'd learned. This hadn't gone like I'd imagined— a happy reunion with Lyric. Not only was she not here, I was now aware of how much danger she was really in. So many things made more sense now.

Mom must have known about Lyric being andeo. Some kind of goddess. That's why she was always so careful about Lyric's eyes.

I remembered mom having Lyric wear normal-colored contacts on rare occasions when we had to travel—I'd forgotten about that. Mom had been so nonchalant about it. Acted like she just didn't want extra attention.

Mom's 'no pictures' rules.

How we were always on the move.

My shoulders sagged, and I looked down at my hands.

I had seriously failed in following mom's footsteps. I'd gotten lax and complacent.

Even after I took Lyric home, I was going to have to redouble the efforts to keep her safe. I would have to put art school on hold, again. Maybe give up that dream altogether. The thought caused a lump to form in my throat—it felt so devastatingly final.

I shook my head. I couldn't allow myself to think about that.

We've already been in Kansas City for too long.

I resolved to get back to living carefully. Stay on the move.

At least I see the threat clearly now.

Plans for Lyric's safety developed in my head.

This is manageable with some sacrifice and hard work.

After my shower and clean clothes, I brushed my dark hair, looking in the mirror. I looked fierce, like a soldier. The clothes fit and were comfortable, though I wasn't willing to test the fireproof ability. My brain was still working on

solutions to every scenario I could think of where Lyric
needed protecting.

*I need to master this magic. It will make all the difference
in keeping her safe. Why did I squander my opportunity to
learn what Kai knows?*

I slammed the brush down and scooped up the clothes
I'd borrowed from Kai, giving them a quick scrub with soap
and water in the sink. I didn't know how plumbing worked
here, but whether it was magic or technology, I was grateful
that it operated similar enough to what I was used to at
home.

Once the Dragonborn's clothes were clean and wrung out as
best I could, I set off to find him. The heap of wet clothes
heavy under one arm. I'd thought about drying them with
the heat from my fire magic, but I didn't want to risk
destroying anything on this rebel base.

He can dry his own clothes.

I found Kai, still shirtless, working on restitching his
armor belt where one part had been damaged. His work was
steady and precise. Someone less intimidating might have
looked a little soft with a sewing needle, but the dragonborn
looked as battle hardened as ever.

I dropped the wet clothes on the floor next to his chair.
"I washed them."

He narrowed his eyes at the pile. "Are you going to dry
them?"

Ignoring his question, I cocked my hip. "Can you train
me in red magic?"

I noticed his gaze travel up my body and dart to my face.

His eyes hadn't lingered. I suddenly felt inadequate and my face heated. I chided myself for being affected by him.

He went back to his task. "Dry my clothes."

I folded my arms. "You said yourself, I need training."

He didn't look up. "After dinner."

"Wait, is that a yes?"

Finally, his eyes met mine. He raised his eyebrows. It looked like he was about to say something, but instead he closed his eyes and gave a small growl.

I nodded once. "After dinner."

I had no bandwidth for his mood swings, so I turned and walked away.

Whatever. I don't need him to like me. I just need him to help me train.

I ignored him when he called out for me to dry his clothes.

THIRTEEN

I met up with Tyler who was just coming out of the men's shower room. He wore camo, similar to what the guards had been wearing. We headed to the dining hall, along with a couple of rebels trailing behind us. It kind of felt like we were being subtly monitored everywhere we went. I was just grateful that they trusted us enough to feed us and let us stay here.

My stomach rumbled as we sat at one of two long wooden tables, waiting for the occupants of the other table to finish serving at the buffet line.

To my irritation, Freya had seated herself across from me.

"So, you didn't know your sister was andeo?" She leaned forward, crossing her arms on the table.

I was not about to give her any information about me or Lyric. I didn't trust her.

When I didn't respond, she asked another question. "How old is she?"

Tyler said, "She just turned sixteen."

I whipped my head to look at Tyler. "What day is it?"

"Her birthday was yesterday." He shrugged at me.

Oh my gosh. How did I lose track of what day it was?

"How did you keep her hidden all these years?" Freya asked.

I turned to look at the Elven woman with fire in my eyes. "I'm not here to answer your questions."

I glanced at the food line. The savory smell was making my mouth water.

"What's your relationship with the andeo?" Freya was asking Tyler.

I elbowed him and said, "He's not answering your questions either."

Finally, it was our table's turn to get our food. I hauled Tyler with me so he wouldn't talk to the pointy-eared rebel.

I was glad when she fell into line several yards behind us and out of earshot.

"She's awful," I huffed.

Tyler was staring, absent-minded, at the stone floor. He whispered, "Lyric... a goddess..."

"She's still Lyric." I couldn't think about their goddess lore.

"What do you think they meant by her ascending? Like she becomes a goddess? Or is she already a goddess?"

"I don't know," I said. "The whole andeo thing is weird to me."

A light voice came from behind us. "If you have questions about andeo, we actually have a historian on base who is an expert on the subject!"

Tyler and I turned. The girl stuck out her hand with a grin. "I'm Sibel."

She was slight of build and as short as me, her cheerful face framed by flyaway blond curls.

Tyler shook her hand and introduced both of us.

"This is Mateo." Sibel hitched her thumb at the guy next to her.

Mateo nodded in greeting, his tousled sand-color hair falling down his forehead.

"So are you guys really from the Realm of Stars?" The unabashed curiosity in Sibel's voice was endearing.

Tyler shrugged. "Yeah, I guess that's what they call it."

Sibel gave Mateo an excited look before turning back to us. "I can't believe I get to meet you!"

"Here we go," Mateo said.

"What!" She swatted her companion before returning to her fangirling. "Okay, my dad was stationed there a couple of times for the rebels when I was little. He would bring back such cool stories and strange tech."

We stepped forward as the line ebbed closer to the serving table and Sibel kept talking. "I would love to visit there. Did you guys live close to Greece?"

Tyler explained where Kansas City was in relation to Europe. "The closest I've been to Greece is a gyro from City Market, and the Neptune Fountain on the Plaza."

"Okay, but that little Greek cafe at City Market is amazing," I said. Willing the line to move faster so we could eat.

Finally, it was our turn, and I loaded my bowl with what looked like buttery little potatoes and a vegetable broth, along with a big hunk of torn off bread—which somehow made the bread seem more delicious than if it had been sliced.

"Wanna sit with us?" Sibel offered.

"Lead the way," I said. At least I didn't have to sit with Freya.

As we ate, we discovered that Sibel and Mateo were part of the tech team for the rebels. They were in charge of comms, and video feed, and some of the security gear. It was all run on magic, making our tech back home seem cumbersome in comparison, with it's need for wires and batteries.

"What I'd really like to do is find a way to make hybrid tech from the stuff you guys use on your earth, combined with the stuff we use on ours," Sibel said. "I think it would really give us an advantage. But the Realm of Stars tech is outlawed here because Alifar is power hungry and doesn't like anyone to travel there unless it's on his terms. We've always smuggled a few things back and forth, but I dream of a day when we could just innovate without fear."

With that, Tyler found his tribe amongst the rebels. Being a computer hacker back on earth, he had a lot to say on the matter. The three of them, energetic and excited, talked shop while I filled my belly.

What if they're all right about Lyric being andeo? The evidence made a compelling argument. I wanted to understand without talking to Freya.

If I can understand it, I can work on figuring out how to protect Lyric from the dangers that come with it.

Once I was finished eating, I selfishly inserted myself into their conversation. "Hey, can I ask you guys a question?"

"Sure!" Sibel said.

"I don't need expert level knowledge. I just was hoping you could tell me the basics about the andeo race."

"What do you want to know?"

"Just pretend I know nothing and summarize."

"Okay." Sibel looked up in thought before meeting my eyes again. "Andeo are the precursor of The Goddess."

"And who is the goddess?"

"Well, here we know her as The Goddess. In your realm, they call the goddess Mother Earth. She's the conduit for the magic of the realm. The key to all the power that flows through."

"Okay." It seemed kind of vague to me, and the confusion must have shown in my expression.

Sibel continued. "Think of it like there's a river of magic flowing through the universe, but the earth can't access it without the conduit of The Goddess."

"Mother Earth has been around since... forever so why are there andeo now?"

"The Goddess is not just one being that lives on forever. She retires eventually, and as she fades away is reincarnated anew." Sibel gestured as she spoke, using her hands as props for her explanation. "That's when a new andeo is born and when they reach physical maturity, they ascend."

Okay, so I need to prevent ascension. I started my mental checklist.

"How long do they stay goddesses for?" Tyler asked.

"It's different every time. Some can work as the conduit for hundreds of years. Ours has been the same for almost two centuries."

"How do you know?"

"When there's a change of the goddess, the ritual sends a

pulse of magic through the entire realm and everyone can feel it…" Sibel shrugged. "You just know. No one alive today has ever experienced it."

"Except Alifar," Mateo said before popping some bread into his mouth.

Sibel nodded. "Yeah, he's been using the Realm of Stars andeo to keep himself powerful and young for thousands of years."

Keep Lyric out of Alifar's reach.

"How?" Tyler asked.

"He finds them when they reincarnate, and he sacrifices them to take their power."

"Some say he drinks the silver from their eyes," Mateo added.

I shuddered. *So gross.*

Sibel nodded. "He has unmatched amounts of power and can draw from the earth any kind of magic he wants to use. It's what makes him so hard to beat."

"I thought I heard some of the other rebels say he's weakened right now," Tyler said.

"Yeah, because he hasn't been able to find the andeo."

"Is there only one?" I asked.

"One for each realm at a time."

Tyler and I looked at each other.

"Lyric?" Tyler sounded as skeptical as I was.

I couldn't quite believe that this entity they were talking about was my little sister.

I helped Mom potty train her.

"Who's Lyric?" Sibel's eyebrows knit together.

"It's her sister," Tyler said, nodding his head toward me.

"She's the reason we're here." I cut Tyler off. "We're trying to find her."

I knew some rebels knew about Lyric but didn't want everyone knowing that my sister was the one and only andeo this guy was looking for. Especially since Freya had already suggested killing Lyric would solve the rebel's problems.

I turned to Sibel, wanting to get her talking again. "So, he's been looking for this specific andeo for—?"

She looked back and forth between Tyler and I, clearly trying to make sense of our little aside before continuing. "Well, he's always tracking down the newest R.O.S andeo. There was a small rebel force that intercepted this last one when she was first reincarnated."

Mateo leaned forward putting his elbows on the table. "It was legendary. There was a huge battle."

"Yeah!" Sibel took over, her blond curls bouncing as she became more animated. "Alifar sent his lackeys to get her, but we had a force that got there in time to stop him. A total bloodbath. No one came back alive."

"But Alifar didn't end up with the andeo," Mateo said, shrugging. "So we're pretty sure one of our people survived long enough to get her to safety."

A memory, hazy and long buried, flooding my mind.

A pit had formed in my stomach.

"The blood." It came out as a whisper.

Lyric really was this andeo they were all talking about.

"What?" Tyler asked.

"Nothing." I glanced between the three of them, forcing a smile.

I need to train while I can, and get out of this place, so I can find my sister.

"I just have some work to do." I stood.

"It was really nice to meet you!" Sibel's smile was warm and genuine.

I could almost imagine her being my friend.

In that moment, I realized I hadn't allowed myself to have any close friends in a very long time. I thought of Jen from the diner. She had been great, but I'd kept her at a distance. I never truly let anyone in. Friendship required a certain amount of trust, and I was too wary to trust anyone.

Friends would be nice.

I squared my shoulders and excused myself to find Kai.

Don't get distracted.

Tyler followed me across the room. When we were almost to the door, he pulled my arm to stop me. "Astrid what was that?"

"What?"

"You looked scared and mentioned blood." His brown eyes narrowed. "You can't leave a guy hanging like that."

I glanced around. No one was paying attention to us. "I think someone brought Lyric to my mom." I shook my head. "I thought it was a bad dream I had when I was young."

"What happened?" Tyler leaned in.

"It—it was the middle of the night." I looked down at the stone floor, trying to remember specifics. "Mom told me to hide in my room. She said she would be right back, like hide-and-seek."

I traced a pattern on the stone with the toe of my boot, feeling too exposed. I'd never spoken of this 'dream' aloud.

My stomach clenched at the images in my head. "I was scared. I think I must have heard something... I knew I wasn't supposed to, but I peeked out."

"What was it?" He was engrossed.

"There was a man and a baby, both covered in blood." I shuddered.

"Do you think he was a rebel?" Tyler asked, drawing the same conclusion I had.

"I don't know. I just remember being terrified of him. And knew that I would get in trouble if they saw me, so I hid in my bed under the covers until I fell asleep."

"Does Lyric know this part of her story?" Tyler's eyes narrowed. "She's never mentioned it to me."

I shook my head. "Like I said—until now, I thought I'd dreamed the whole thing... Maybe I did dream it." I shrugged. "When my mom introduced me to my new sister, it seemed like a completely different time in my memory. My mom was happy, and I was excited. There was definitely no blood."

"Well, your mom was a saint to take in a baby for a stranger." He squeezed my arm. "I bet she didn't realize the danger you guys were all going to be in."

I shook my head. "There are so many things I wish I could ask her."

"I'm sorry."

"It's okay..." I tossed my chin toward Sibel and Mateo who were chatting. "You should hang out. I'm going to find Kai and do some training."

I was just outside the dining hall when I felt a light touch on my back. "Ready?"

I startled, turning to find the dragonborn at my shoulder. "Jeez! You're like a shadow."

Kai was wearing his clothes that I'd borrowed. They were clean and dry. I cocked an eyebrow at him. "I was just coming to find you."

"I know. I heard."

I gave him a flat look. "Just because you can hear well doesn't mean it's okay to listen to people's private conversations."

He ignored me and started walking down the hall to the left. "I found one of their sparring rooms."

I rolled my eyes at his back and followed.

He led me to a large open room with rows of crates at the edges. In the center, Kai set up the discs that created the training circle. When it shimmered to life, and wasn't filled with darkness, I smiled a little.

We stepped into the circle and I took a strong stance. Ready to make as much progress as possible.

"Bring your red light out and just restrain it in your hands," He instructed. "Focus on maintaining control."

The grounding shoes were incredible. I could feel the flow of magic through them from the natural stone floor.

I brought the red light up through me, and fire filled the dome.

When the fire died, I looked down, my shoulders sagging in relief.

My clothes were indeed fireproof.

Kai coached me on getting my power to submit. I tried to manage it. Over and over I failed. Over and over, I tried again, determined to succeed. It was well into the night when Kai told me it was time to give it a rest.

I shook my head. "I'm going to master this."

He tilted his head towards me. "It doesn't have to be conquered in one day."

"I don't have more time," I snapped. "I need to get it now."

"Red light is by far the hardest magic to master." Kai summoned a flame and held it in his hand. "This represents years of practice."

"Things are more dangerous than I realized." I balled my hands into fists. "I need to use all my resources to protect my sister."

Kai closed his palm, snuffing out the flame. "Okay." He nodded, understanding coming across his face. "Let's go again."

At least he understood that.

After long hours of doggedly trying to create a small precise flame instead of an explosion, I'd made very little progress.

I sat on the floor trembling with fatigue. Kai extended a hand. I took it and allowed him to pull me to my feet.

We were standing close and he had to bend his head to look into my face. "You have to learn to control your emotions."

I threw my hands up. "I am!"

Ugh! He's so not helpful.

He placed a gentle hand on my shoulder. "When your emotions are heightened, it's harder to control what the magic is doing. It becomes unpredictable."

"Well, I can't just flip the off switch on all my feelings," I said, pacing the floor. "Even if I could, no offense, but I don't want to be you."

He looked off into the distance for a moment. I braced myself for his retort.

His tone was rigid when he spoke. "We'll try again tomorrow."

"We're quitting because I pointed out that you're emotionally constipated?" I threw my hands up, my tone mocking. "I didn't realize that was going to offend you."

"You're frustrated, and you need rest." He walked over and bent to retrieve one of the discs for the training circle.

Had I been rational, I would have recognized and been grateful for the boon he offered. Rest. Knowing that we would not give up.

I kept complaining. "Why is this so hard?"

Kai jerked his head in the direction of the door. "Let's go."

The way the motion made his hair brush against his shoulders reminded me of the warrior braid that was no longer there.

The braid he had traded to save my life.

My shoulders fell.

It wasn't his fault that I couldn't master my magic.

I felt a little guilty for taking my frustration out on him. Though I inwardly maintained my stance that he was mostly unfeeling, I let go of my pride just enough to stalk off to bed.

FOURTEEN

Morning came after a night of dead-to-the-world kind of sleep. I felt renewed for the first time in what seemed like endless days of travel and peril. Kai, Tyler, and I headed to a bunker with two rebels, Hiram Brewhood, the Halfling from the day before; and Freya Cardalan, the cold Elven historian, who I'd started to think of as public enemy number one.

The bunker was outside of the caves and one of several large structures with rounded rooftops. The rebels seemed skilled at camouflage, because the buildings were painted to blend in with the lush surrounding foliage. Or maybe it was a spell.

Stepping into the enormous building that housed the ship we were going to take, I felt tiny. We approached a ship that was flat on the bottom and oval on the sides. The rows of seating reminded me of a bus with no top. It had a glossy brown finish with subtle purple hues, mimicking some trees I'd seen in the forests in this realm. The vessel was big but it felt dwarfed in the building.

Two rebels were working on the ship—a pair of twins with the same last name on their uniforms: Shalo. They didn't seem to ever speak, yet they worked in perfect rhythm with each other as they prepped to sail.

Tyler tried to introduce himself to one twin. When he got no response, he sat down next to me with a shrug.

"Ezra is a divider," Hiram said. "One is only a copy of the other."

"Woah, cloning abilities?" Tyler sounded impressed.

"His ability to divide himself lets him get more done. But I'm told it takes a great deal of concentration." Hiram nodded towards Ezra. "That's why dividers don't speak when they're using their ability."

"That is so cool!" Tyler wore a huge grin. "Dude, I love it here."

Large bay doors opened and morning sun flooded the bunker. One of the Ezra's placed a fist-size, glowing yellow stone into a cradle on the hull of the ship, and the vessel rose off the ground.

I looked over the side at the ground several feet below us. My stomach flipped with excitement and nerves.

We pulled out of the large doors. The wind rushed past as we sped along, following a path through the trees that was just large enough for the ship to glide through. To my relief, we never flew much higher than a few feet off the ground.

I closed my eyes and tipped my head back, letting the wind kiss my face. The edges of my mouth lifted.

The speed felt like real progress towards finding Lyric.

Kai sat in the back of the vessel and hadn't looked at me or spoken to me all morning. I guess he was in a bad mood after my outburst from the night before. I had behaved rudely, but I didn't plan on making amends.

I wasn't completely wrong in what I said. The guy has issues.

I ignored him. A hired body guard doesn't have to be a friend, they just have to do their job.

Eventually, we came out of the forest landscape and passed a few towns. There were other flying vessels and lots of people living their lives, just like on our Earth. I saw children laughing and playing, mothers hanging the wash out to dry, and people gathered casually in conversation. They all seemed oblivious to our ship, whose purpose was to intercede events that could change the fate of their realm forever.

Tyler scooted closer to me on the bench to talk to me over the wind. "I realized last night that it's because of this Alifar guy that our earth is completely cut off from all this magic." He gestured around at the thriving metropolis we were passing.

"Yeah, that's what it sounded like," I said.

"And Lyric is the person who can heal the earth."

"Over my dead body." I cut him off, not wanting to hear the rest of his thought.

"When Lyric finds out, you know she's going to want to fix this."

You think I don't know that?

The thought alone was making me sick with worry.

"She's not going to find out." My tone was firm.

"Astrid, it's her passion."

"No." I shook my head. "We find her, we get her home. End of story."

"But Alifar is hunting her."

I'd already thought about that too.

"We know how to disappear. I will keep her safe."

"You're going to leave Kansas City?"

I looked away. Wind filled the silence.

"I'll come with you," Tyler said.

"What about your mom? And school?"

"I had enough credits to graduate last semester. And my mom has been telling me to move out and quit living on her dime ever since."

"You're only seventeen!" I resented Tyler's mom and stepdad for how lame they were to him. He was a good guy.

Tyler shrugged. "I'm ready to get out. I only stayed because I've been waiting for Lyric."

"Tyler..." My heart hurt for him. "You know she cares about you."

"I know."

"But it's never going to be romantic."

"Hey, you let me worry about myself." He put an arm around my shoulder. "I'm going to help you guys."

I'd never have a brother, but I thought this must be pretty close to what it would be like.

"Okay." I finally relented. "You can come."

He did a little fist pump.

"But I don't want you telling Lyric about the ascension stuff."

"Don't you think she has a right to know?"

"The next andeo can bring magic back to the earth after Lyric has lived a full, vibrant life." They couldn't have my sister.

Tyler shook his head. But he said, "Okay."

. . .

We traveled for several hours. I was grateful for the speed and not having to walk. We passed through countryside, and towns, and countryside again. It was fascinating to me to see what was so close to being a familiar landscape, like the rolling hills and endless trees of Missouri, yet different. As an artist, the depth of colors in this realm filled me with curiosity and admiration.

Finally, we stopped just inside the town of Sasca.

The town was not what I had expected. The streets were made of mud. Well I am sure it was dirt, but there must have been rain recently. It reminded me of a good old western. Which reminded me of how much Lyric loved Friday night movie night.

Oh Lyric... please be ok.

I wondered what Lyric had thought of this town. The buildings were a mismatch of some wooden cabin-type structures and some more contemporary buildings with stucco siding in different shades. The shapes of some houses and stores were rounded and hobbit-esque. It was definitely not like the architecture we see on Earth with the almost exclusive use of straight lines. This scene would make for an interesting painting.

This whole world was a contradiction. They had such advanced resources like magic, flying ships, and fireproof clothing. Yet they seemed to live so simply and more at one with the Earth.

Ezra returned to his single form and took the wind stone out of the ship very slowly, which caused the vessel to lower gently to the ground.

I guess there's an art to using wind rocks.

Hiram and Freya left on foot to talk to Ro's family. Ezra

was instructed to stay and monitor us and the ship. He said he would, but as soon as the other two rebels were gone, he plopped down in the grass under the shade of a tree and closed his eyes.

"Apparently it's nap time," Tyler said with a snort. "Hey, where's he going?"

I turned to see Kai striding in the opposite direction that the rebels had gone.

"Kai!" I called after him. He held up a hand in a noncommittal wave without turning around. Then he disappeared around the corner of a building.

I shook my head, turning back to Tyler. "Apparently he's ditching us."

"He'll be back, right?"

Irritated and antsy, I sat down with my back propped against the side of the ship, picking at the grass. "Who cares?"

"Um, I do," Tyler said. "He agreed that if I gave him partial payment, he would see the job through."

I scanned Tyler's arms for my mother's cuff. It wasn't there. "Did you pay him?" Irritation flared in my chest.

"I'm not that stupid," He said, rolling up his sleeve to reveal the cuff still on his wrist. "I kept part of it back."

The stone was missing from its place in the leather.

Unbelievable.

I closed my eyes and leaned my head back against the ship. "You have got to be kidding me."

I breathed through my nose, urging my temper to calm. I could feel my red magic roiling, and I couldn't deal with that right now.

When I opened my eyes, Tyler was looking down at the

cuff on his arm, nodding slowly. "The stone was the only valuable piece, wasn't it?"

"How are you only just realizing that?"

"Okay, in hindsight, that's very obvious." He held up his hands, his freckled face flushing red. "But just listen."

"I don't even want to hear it, Tyler." I closed my eyes and massaged my temples. "We'll find Lyric without that asshole."

Tyler fell silent.

Good. A very good decision on his part.

Tyler was an idiot. But if I was honest, my anger was at Kai's betrayal. I hadn't liked the dragonborn at the start, but he'd proven helpful to have around. I'd gotten used to him. He was this solid, stable presence.

Last night, it had felt like we were starting to understand each other. He'd seemed to appreciate my need to protect Lyric.

And now I'll have to train myself. ...somehow.

Whatever. I'll be fine on my own.

This is just a reminder that I shouldn't rely on anyone else.

People betray and leave.

When I opened my eyes, ready to channel my anger into telling Tyler off for being a fool, he wasn't there.

Nope. He doesn't get to just walk off and not get a lecture.

I got up and stormed around the side of the ship to find him.

A pair of green goblin hands grabbed me. Alarm shot through my veins.

Jalak.

How did they find us?

I screamed. A goblin shoved something sour into my mouth. I thrashed back, trying to spit it out. Three Jalak held me. They slammed me into the side of the ship. The thing they'd put in my mouth had the texture of a root ball covered in sludge. I gagged and writhed. My body trying to puke up whatever slime was trickling down my throat. I tried to spit it out, but a large green hand held it in place.

Tyler lay in a heap on the ground.

My body heaved. I struggled and kicked. The goblins held me firm. My vision blurred.

I reached for my red magic. When I called it out, flame sputtered erratically. One Jalak began burning. He screamed and rolled on the ground while his fellow goblins ignored his cries. The grass near Tyler's prone body lit.

Oh my god, Tyler!

"No! Help him!" My plea to no one was ignored by everyone.

The Jalak carried me away from the ship. My limbs started to feel heavy and numb. Panic filled my mind. My magic was going to kill Tyler, and I hadn't even freed myself.

I tried to struggle. My chest heaving and gagging again. I was being shoved into a large box made of some kind of plastic. I found my red light again. This time, it fizzled with only a spark.

One of the Jalak tied a gag around my head to replace the hand that held the ball of sludge in my mouth. Bile rose in my throat.

I got an arm free and clawed at the eyes of the nearest Jalak. He slammed a fist into my face. My vision blacked. They yanked my arm behind my back and tied my hands together before shoving me the rest of the way into the box.

The box closed, and darkness enveloped me. Emptiness filled my core. I searched for my magic. I couldn't find it. I recognized this box felt like the room at the rebel base that had been spelled to suppress magic.

I thrashed against the box as panic overtook every rational thought.

Swallowed by the darkness, I couldn't hear anything from outside of the box. My limbs finally became completely numb and could no longer even thrash against my prison.

The box opened and light poured in. I blinked up to see a scowl on Kai's face.

My body sagged in relief and confusion.

Kai reached in and hauled me from my prison, setting me on my feet. When my legs buckled, he only just kept me from hitting the ground.

I was slumped in the dirt next to a dead Jalak.

The dragonborn untied my gag. I spit the ball of crap out of my mouth, coughing and hacking.

And then I puked.

Kai growled. "Why do I keep having to save your ass?"

I retched again. Kai held me up.

When I finally had nothing left in my stomach, I cried. Tears mixed with the blood that was trickling down my face.

"I killed Tyler." My voice was a hoarse whisper.

He was unconscious. There's no way he didn't get burnt.

I can't be trusted with this magic.

"Well, there are worse things that could have happened to him." Kai's expression was all business as he sheathed a knife I didn't realize he'd been holding.

"Is that supposed to make me feel better?"

"Sorry. I know you cared about him." His tone didn't convey much sympathy.

"You are not a very nice person." I scowled from my place on the ground.

"I keep telling you that." He shrugged.

The fact that he had just saved me was obviously a point in his favor, but I also knew he didn't do it just to be nice, so I wasn't sure if it fully counted.

"Oh good! You're back!" Kai and I both turned at the sound of the familiar voice. Tyler was limping towards us, holding his bleeding, blackened head. Half of his red hair was singed away.

"Tyler!" My voice came out a rasp. His clothes were half burned, and he had third-degree blisters on the right side of his face and arm. I felt sick knowing I'd caused them.

"You're still alive?" Kai said, disbelief clear.

"Don't sound so disappointed. I might think you don't like me." Tyler smiled, his teeth bright in contrast to his sooty face.

"Tyler, I'm so, so sorry." I started to cry again.

"Hey, it's okay." Tyler waved a hand like it was no big deal. "Just maybe you could try one of those orange balls of light on my face?" He winced, trying to hide it from me. "Because it hurts like the son of a motherless donkey."

I chuckled once and nodded. "Yeah." I swallowed the lump in my throat. "Yeah, of course."

"Let's get out of here before the Jalak find us again." Tyler glanced around.

"That was the only patrol around." Kai said as he scooped my still-numb body off the ground.

"How do you know?" I said.

"I checked."

Oh.

I let out a breath.

Part of me wanted to be annoyed at the close contact, but since he'd carried me on the long flight before, all I felt was secure.

"Hey, where did you go?" Tyler asked as we walked.

"I had business to take care of."

"We thought you took the stone and left." Tyler was still gripping his injured head.

"I told you—I'm an assassin, not a thief."

I still thought his moral compass was kind of screwy. But I was deeply grateful that 'save people from the goblins' was apparently included in his creed.

Since Tyler wasn't dead, I was feeling a little more charitable towards the dragonborn.

"Thanks for getting me out of that box," I said.

Kai's chest rumbled with a low growl, in response.

When we got back to the ship, it was being consumed by flames.

My heart sank.

There goes our exit strategy.

There was a crowd of people watching as the vessel burned. Two people were working with their blue light magic to douse the flames. I spotted Ezra—who was only one Ezra —standing near the fire fighters. He looked pissed. I prayed no one would know it was my magic that started the fire.

Kai carried me to the shade of a nearby tree. As he lowered me to the grass, our eyes met. His were dark and full of something intense that unnerved me. I was suddenly aware of my chest rising and falling as our breath mingled.

His now familiar scent of pine and musk flooded my senses.

This man is so attractive it almost hurts to look at him.

My mind replayed the kiss we had shared in the fae forest. I both hoped and worried he was about to repeat it. Warning bells were sounding in my mind. *No distractions, Astrid. Keep your guard up.*

I looked away and cleared my throat. "Thanks."

He stepped away from me, and I was glad of the space.

I turned my attention to the burning ship. Efforts to put out the flames were in full force. Once the fire was out, the firefighters took a statement from Ezra. He hadn't seen what happened. They also wanted a statement from Tyler and I. We blamed the Jalak for the fire.

Eventually, the four of us—Tyler, Kai, Ezra, and I—sat in the shade of a large flowering tree and stared at the blackened half-a-ship that was left. My extremities were tingly, but becoming less numb.

Eventually, Freya and Hiram came back. They were pissed about the ship but didn't spend much time dwelling on it.

Freya turned to Ezra. "Get a new ship here. Now."

Ezra nodded and started off.

"What did you find out?" I asked, anxious for news of Lyric's whereabouts.

"Alifar took Ro's daughter," Hiram said.

Ezra stopped in his tracks and turned around, disbelief written in every feature.

"What does that mean?" Tyler looked back and forth between the rebels.

"We don't know yet." Hiram folded his dwarf arms in defiance.

"It means..." Freya glared at the halfling. "That Ro has likely betrayed us."

Hiram's fists balled. "We don't know that for sure."

"We have to assume that the High Lord either already has the andeo, or soon will." Freya turned to Ezra again. "Get that ship. I already called in to Commander Dia. We have orders to meet the rebel force on the way to the High Lord's keep."

"We're attacking now?" Ezra was wide eyed. "I thought we were trying to let him weaken for one more year."

"Now that he's got his hands on an andeo, our window of opportunity closes tomorrow night."

Ezra nodded in understanding and ran off.

I turned to Freya, trying to keep the panic out of my voice. "Why tomorrow night? What happens then?"

"The andeo sacrifice has to be done on a triple full moon, and the next time that happens is tomorrow night."

My stomach dropped.

I have to save her in time.

Fifteen

Kai stood and pulled a small square of cloth out of his pocket and placed it in Tyler's hand. "This is where we part ways, kid."

"Wait, you're not coming?"

"I told you. I don't contract jobs that directly oppose the High Lord."

What? We need you!

"But what about the cuff?" I said. Desperate to keep him from leaving again.

"It's not worth dying for," Kai said. He held my gaze for an extra beat before he turned and launched himself into the air. I didn't even see his broad shadowy wings until he was far above me.

I tore my eyes from the sky where the dragonborn receded into the distance, trying to tamp down the rising panic in my chest.

Of course he left. What else did I expect from him?

I was tired of the emotional whiplash he seemed to

constantly create. This was exactly why it was best to keep him at a safe distance.

Tyler unwrapped the cloth in his hand. Inside it lay the magic suppression stone from my cuff.

"He... he's gone," Tyler said. "What do we do?"

The look on his face begged for reassurance. I didn't know how to give it to him. I turned away.

"Astrid, we can't do this without him."

Fierce resolve pierced through my hurt and despair. "Yes," I snapped. "We can. ...We have to."

"We just need a plan." I looked up at Tyler's blackened face. "Let's start by cleaning up those burns while we're waiting for the ship."

I gestured for Tyler to lie on the grass. He did so, gingerly.

"You're a healer?" Hiram asked.

"I... yep." I wasn't sure who to trust with knowledge of my second power.

A healer. I like that.

The thought calmed me. I thought of Lyric. I imagined the moment I would get to tell her I could heal her for good. Hope began to subdue my fears.

I figured out healing on my own. I can figure out fire. It'll just take time.

Kai could leave. We didn't need him.

I turned my attention to the task at hand. Tyler's burns were the worst on his face and arms. My stomach clenched with shame at having done this to him.

"It would be better to save your strength for the battle ahead." Freya watched me with her arms folded and the usual scowl on her face.

I rolled my eyes and said to Tyler. "Don't worry, I'm not going to let you suffer like this."

Now that my body wasn't numb, I could sense my magic —a relief after being without it for even the short time. I'd come to find some comfort in the light inside me, even when I wasn't actively using it.

Grounded to the earth so I could draw on its power, I took a few calming breaths and concentrated on the orange light in my core. 'Heal him like it never happened' was the chant in my head.

Drawing on the orange light and scooping it up into a glowing orb, I repeated the chant mentally as I pressed the light into the side of Tyler's head that was the most injured.

I went back to my core to find more orange light and summoned another round of healing magic. This time, I sank the magic into his arm and side. The light entered him and fused with his body, causing him to glow briefly before fading.

I used a third orb of light on his legs. I wasn't sure what damage had been done, but I was determined to be thorough and fix what I had broken.

"That's a lot of magic," Hiram warned. "Even for a grounded healer."

I shrugged. "I want to make sure he's ready to face tomorrow at full strength."

"A waste," Freya scoffed. "Now you won't be at full strength for the battle."

"Don't worry about me." It was my magic to use, not hers.

"I'm worried because I don't want you slowing us down," She said. "We don't need any more liabilities."

Tyler opened his mouth to say something, and I put my hand up to stop him. "You don't move until this is done."

I ignored the rebels and smiled at Tyler.

He closed his eyes and took a breath that spoke of relief and surrender.

I felt a rush of gratitude that Lyric and Tyler had become friends.

Because of that friendship, I'm not alone out here.

I sat with him for a long time like that, silently watching the blisters on his skin recede. Even his singed red hair grew back.

His face was still dirty, but he became completely healed. Wonder lifted my heart. It was amazing. I didn't think it would ever get old, watching the miracle happen before my eyes.

Healing Tyler had been draining, but I didn't regret it. I let the power of the earth soak into my soul as I sat on the ground. It renewed me little by little.

Tyler's injuries didn't take nearly as long as the dragon's wing had—maybe because these were surface wounds, maybe because his entire body was smaller than the one dragon wing. Maybe because I'd put a lot more intention behind the magic, as I'd felt desperate to make Tyler whole.

By the time Ezra was back with a working ship, Tyler was ready to climb aboard.

This ship was much smaller than the last one and made of metal. It had wear and tear, but it looked kind of like a torpedo. I hoped that meant it was fast.

We were soon speeding along to meet up with the rebel attack force.

. . .

The new ship was very fast. Beautiful scenery flew by.

I couldn't watch it. "I feel sick."

"Motion sickness?" Tyler asked.

"I'm just so worried." I rubbed my arm where my cuff used to be, longing for the comfort I used to find there. "We might be heading to our deaths. You should have stayed with Gemma where it's safe."

Tyler bumped my shoulder. "And let you get all the credit for rescuing the fair maiden?" He puffed up his chest a bit and added, "I'm the one with a mind-link to a pet dragon, so I'd say I'm pretty well equipped to be the hero at this point."

I smiled, but it soon faded back to worry. "What if I can't protect her?"

"You can't." The voice came from the row behind us.

I whipped my head around to where Freya sat. Her resting scowl accentuated the fact that she was an awful person.

"Then I'll die trying." I glared at her.

The Elven woman shrugged. "The only way to make an andeo truly safe is for them to ascend."

I turned away from her. "Don't pay attention to her, Tyler. We don't need that kind of negativity." I took a deep breath and exhaled slowly, like I was in a training session. "We'll be fine. We just have to get her home."

I tried to sound confident—I had to convince myself.

"What if she's right?" Tyler fiddled with a button on his jacket.

"She's not." My response was quick. I couldn't even look at that idea long enough to consider it. I squared my shoulders. "Let's go over our plan again."

. . .

We met up with the rebels outside of the capital city. From our vantage point on a hill, we could see the sprawling metropolis nestled in a huge valley. It was laid out like a wagon wheel. Low-lying buildings covered the basin. In the center, the dark spires of the High Lord's tower loomed far above the rest of the city and cast long menacing shadows over everything in its wake. My stomach was fraught with nerves.

Sibel and Mateo greeted us. They didn't seem to share the somber attitude of some of the rebels. Their energy spoke of nervous excitement. An event they've all been preparing for, finally come to be.

"Does your sister really have bright silver eyes?" Sibel asked.

I nodded.

Mateo whistled—the sound a poetic curse.

"And you really didn't know about Andeo before?" Her blonde curls bounced as she shook her head in disbelief.

"We really didn't." I shrugged.

"Well, you are about to witness history!" Sibel announced. "A lot of us have been preparing our whole adult lives for this moment."

"Here." Mateo motioned for us to step over to a large trunk full of black fabric. "Grab yourself a disguise."

Sibel said, "We've been making replicas of the guard uniforms so we can infiltrate the castle with fewer casualties."

Tyler pulled out a folded black jumpsuit with a royal crest. "Nice!"

"If you wear them, you can sneak in and hopefully find your sister while we're keeping the guards busy at the front gate." Mateo gestured to the box. "Astrid, try one on."

I pulled out a dark robe that had a cowl on it. The black fabric flickered. It felt magical. It reminded me of a wizard robe. I smiled, thinking Lyric would appreciate the look.

As I was putting my arms in the holes to try it on, Sibel jumped back. "Whoa! Be careful with that!"

"Oh, sorry," I said, shrugging it off.

"Wait." Mateo peered at me. "It didn't burn you when you put it on?"

"No," I said, shrugging and trying to hand the special cloak to Sibel. Wanting to get rid of it as quickly as possible.

She stepped back. "I can't even touch that."

I examined the fabric in my hand more closely. It definitely exuded power. A shiver of nerves rippled through me.

"No one can touch that with without gloves." Mateo was eyeing me.

"Even with gloves, I wouldn't risk it," Sibel added.

"Maybe Astrid can because she has magic from a different realm?" Tyler suggested.

"That could be." Mateo's expression relaxed a little.

"Whatever the reason..." Sibel gave a small chuckle. "You just found yourself a way in with the High Lord."

"What is this thing?" I asked unfurling the glinting fabric.

"It's the uniform of Alifar's inner circle, his team of sorcerers and witches who protect him at all times."

"Several rebels sacrificed their lives to get that, only to find that no one can use it," Mateo said.

"It's spelled with some kind of protection so that no one can wear it and impersonate an inner circle member." Sibel shuddered. "If you can wear it, you basically have security clearance all the way to the top."

What does that say about me?

I couldn't think about it.

I put the cloak on. The two rebels watched me expectantly.

"Nothing?"

I shook my head. "It feels fine."

"That is so cool," Mateo said.

"How is a person supposed to fight in this? I kicked inside of the long robe with my toe. "It's so cumbersome."

"I think they mostly do fighting with their magic," Mateo said.

"Oh good." I raised my eyebrows. "I'm infiltrating a den of ruthless sorcerers."

"Just try to blend in." Sibel nodded encouragingly.

I took a deep breath. "Thank you for helping us."

Sibel smiled. "What are friends for?"

"She's hoping that someday, when this is over, you'll let her visit you in your realm." Mateo gave her a teasing look.

She gave a sheepish shrug. "Friends visit friends. That's a normal thing."

"Absolutely, you can visit us!" Tyler said, giving both of them high fives. "We can show you all around Kansas City."

Except we won't be there because we're flying under the radar as soon as we get back.

I didn't think that was worth mentioning because right now we would all be lucky to make it out alive.

"Be careful," I said, nodding towards the ominous castle.

"We are on tech, so we're going to be here at the ship." Mateo patted the exterior.

"Yeah." Sibel fist bumped her friend. "They station us in a remote location, because the operation would be a complete fail without us doing our job."

"Speaking of our job..." Mateo pulled up a holographic map of the ground floor of the castle. "This is the main entrance." He pointed. "But back over here on the east side, there's a tunnel that is not visible to anyone without a spell ring."

"Spell ring?" I asked.

"It's a ring that can contain a certain specific power," Sibel explained. "The High Lord gives them to his favorite courtesans or friends, that he wants coming and going discreetly."

Mateo added, "So you won't be able to see it, but one of our deep undercover people has planted a white rosebush on the north side of it, you'll be able to find it. Then you just have to physically push through the barrier."

"Once you're in, we can't help you, because we don't know where your sister is," Sibel said. "But at least you'll be able to get inside."

"If we have these disguises, couldn't we just walk in the front?" Tyler asked.

"Well, if you do that, you'll be jeopardizing our mission," Sibel said, "so vice commander Neeman wouldn't allow it."

Sibel nodded. "It's the east entrance, or nothing. Sorry, best we can do."

The vice commander was addressing his troops. "Listen up. We have to get in there before Alifar starts the ritual. That means it's go time. Commander Dia is on her way, but she's ordered me to lead the attack now and not wait."

The large man wiped sweat off of his forehead with the

back of his hand as he spoke. "The ritual could start at any point after the moons rise. If that happens, he'll have so much added protection that it'll be impossible to get to him."

Pausing a beat, he looked around at the rebels he was leading. "Does everyone have their orders?"

A hundred rebels saluted in silent affirmation. It seemed like such a small force to take for an attack on a man who made even the dragonborn nervous.

Tyler and I headed for the castle as the rebels made their final preparations. Walking through the streets of the bustling city that surrounded the castle, I realized the rebels would smuggle their smaller band of fighters into position much more easily than if they'd had a larger force. Especially since they were all dressed as guards.

Tyler wore his guard uniform, but I had my cloak tucked into a satchel Sibel had given me. I didn't want to wear it until I had gotten past the shrubbery and into the castle because it was hard to maneuver in.

We ducked into the shadow of a nearby building and waited for some people to pass before we approached the castle. Once the pedestrians had turned onto a different street, I turned to Tyler. "This is it."

His eyes went wide. "Wait, what if we go through this invisible door and there are people right on the other side?"

"We'll just pull the old 'Wookie prisoner trick' and you can tell them you're escorting me to the dungeons."

Tyler smiled. "Nice! I've always wanted to do that." He

looked down at his guard uniform. "Not exactly the uniform I pictured in this scenario, but it works."

Now that we were closer, I could see that the castle was made of what looked like natural stone. As if the spires had been called out of the earth and the slate had risen to obey.

My heart hammered as we approached. The single entrance at the front had been heavily guarded. I hoped the rebels could get through. We had taken the long way around to the side to avoid being seen.

A small white rose bush stood about a quarter way down the side, as promised. Foliage grew thick all around it—not only did there not appear to be a door, but there was no exposed rock either. Acting on faith, I climbed through the bushes, just south of the white roses. Pushing through the leaves and flowers that covered the stone, I pressed my palms onto the wall itself. Nothing happened. There was no sign that there was an opening there. I continued to push harder. Tyler pushed with me.

"Maybe we're on the wrong side of the roses," Tyler said.

He tried the other side of the bush with no success.

Remembering the training force field and how I'd had to gently walk through to get out, I dropped my arms and tried that approach.

Shoulders relaxed, muscles loose.

Walking face first towards the wall, I passed through the barrier and into a hallway that was luxurious though stern.

Lights automatically came on in succession as we walked down the hall. It was like walking through an extravagant mansion magazine, perfectly in order and squeaky clean, but it didn't look lived in.

We'd only taken a few steps when a guard hurried by. He

spotted us right away and did a double take. "What is going on here?"

I slid my hands behind my back as discreetly as I could manage. Tyler took the hint, grabbing my arm. "I'm taking this prisoner to cell block eight, sir."

Oh boy. We should have practiced this.

I worked to keep my expression neutral and bland.

The guard narrowed his eyes and looked Tyler up and down. "What division do you belong to?"

Tyler gave a brief salute. "Squadron four, Sir."

The man scoffed. "Four?"

"Twenty-three," Tyler said, confidently. "Four twenty-three"

The man narrowed his eyes. "Who are you?"

"I am... Tyler, son of Martha, and I'm fairly new to the army."

The soldier raised his hand. The natural stone floor under us heaved and molded around our feet so that we were trapped.

Crap.

Turning to me, the man said. "Explain to me why this soldier can't seem to answer basic questions properly."

"Well..." I swallowed, "It's kind of embarrassing. I put a bit of a spell on him because I was..."

Tyler chopped down on the man's carotid artery with the side of his hand and the man fell to the floor.

The ground did not release us. We were still stuck trying to move our feet without success.

"I've always wanted to see if that would really work!" Tyler smiled down at the man.

"Great. But focus!" I tugged at my feet. "We're still trapped by his magic."

"Yeah, I didn't think that through…" Tyler said. "He'll be awake in about 30 seconds and now our cover is blown."

We yanked and pulled. I even tried to take my boots off. "You could have let me finish my story. Maybe he would have bought it."

"He wouldn't have. It was ridiculous."

"So much for being heroes." I gave up on trying to pull free. Discouraged by how badly things were already going.

"Maybe Sakashi is in the area and could come help us?" Tyler's voice trailed off, full of defeat.

"I have a solution," I said.

"Thank goodness."

"It involves fire…"

"Absolutely not."

"Then what do you have in mind?" I spread my hands wide.

"Anything but fire when I'm literally stuck this close to you!"

"Here." I shoved my satchel into Tyler's arms. "Use this as a shield. If it catches fire, you can ditch it."

"You want me to use a flammable bag as a shield against magic fire?"

"Stop whining." I turned my attention to the soldier on the floor, who was waking up.

"What if the magic still holds us after this guy is dead?"

"I'm banking on the fact that it won't." I angled my body away from Tyler as much as I could without being able to move my feet.

"For the record, I do not approve of this plan," Tyler said from behind the bag.

"That makes two of us." I summoned my red light.

The magic channeled through my hands and burst the soldier into flames, along with the nearby table and accent chairs. However, once it consumed the man, the ground released its hold on us. Tyler and I stumbled back, and he dropped the bag, which was on fire.

I grabbed my disguise out of the burning satchel and stomped out the flames. Blocking out the thought that I'd just killed another person. We didn't have a choice.

"You okay?" I asked.

"I'm good." Tyler waved his hand. "Thank you for not burning me this time."

I put on the cloak and examined it to find no damage.

"Maybe it's fireproof."

"We can hope." I started down the hallway again. "Let's go."

Sixteen

Tyler and I hid in a shadowed corner. Two guards stood at the end of the hall on either side of a large door. I had donned my disguise but I was nervous to test its effectiveness by running into another guard, so we'd been dodging patrols right and left. However, we weren't making any progress finding Lyric because we didn't know where to look.

We were going to run out of time.

I turned to Tyler and whispered. "Okay, let's think..."

"I've been doing that this whole time," Tyler whispered. "I've realized that this was a bad plan."

I gave him the side eye before continuing. "If this guy is about to do the ritual, it's likely that he has Lyric with him."

"Meaning?"

"If we find him..." I shrugged. "A good chance we find her."

"What if you're wrong?"

If I'm wrong, we're dead.

"If I'm wrong, we put ourselves in more danger."

"Great."

I put my hand up. "But we may find a clue about where he's keeping her."

"Maybe she's in the dungeon."

"She's high value to him." I pressed my lips into a frown. "Do you think he would put her there?"

"I don't know." Tyler threw up his hands.

"I don't know either." I took a breath and squared my shoulders. "But I'm going with this idea before I think it through too much and talk myself out of it."

"Would that be a bad thing?" Tyler raised his eyebrows.

I didn't respond.

I pulled up the hood of my cloak to lend me some courage and stepped out to approach the two guards. I wore my most haughty expression. Tyler followed at my flank.

"Excuse me." I tried to sound like I was in charge. "I've been ordered to report to High Lord Alifar, but this idiot doesn't seem to know where he is." I hitched my thumb at Tyler, who I hoped was playing along and looking properly ashamed of himself.

The guards took one look at me and bowed their heads, stammering. One had a balding head and the other looked almost as young as Tyler.

The older one said, "Of course you are meant to be in the inner sanctum, Your Excellency."

Neither of the guards would look at me.

Apparently the rebels aren't the only ones who fear the cloak.

"I can escort you if you wish." The younger guard said, bowing lower. "If you'd like to leave your escort here to guard the door in my place."

"Then let's go!" I clapped my hands twice for effect. "I'm in a hurry."

"Leave the idiot here as my replacement." He motioned for Tyler to stand by the door.

Tyler took his place near the door, only for his grumpy old companion to tell him, "I don't need help guarding here. I was about to send him to the front gate. I've just been informed they're experiencing some activity."

Tyler's eyes widened, but he nodded and turned to leave without breaking character.

Crap.

Splitting up was a terrible idea anyway, but now I had accidentally sent Tyler to the front lines, and fighting for the enemy.

I glanced back as the door closed behind me.

Too late now.

The guard led me through several more rooms and hallways, each protected by more guards than the last.

The guards didn't question my authority, they only bowed their heads as I walked by.

Confidence combined with the right outfit can take a girl places.

I smiled inwardly, despite my trepidation.

You were right Lyric.

We came to an ornate double door. Guards stood across the entire front, barring the way.

"Excuse me," my escort said, moving to step past them.

One guard held out an arm. "No one goes in the inner sanctum until the High Lord comes out. Those are my orders."

"I'm supposed to be in there," I said, staring the man right in the eyes.

The man bowed low. "Forgive me Your Excellency. I did not see you there."

Pretty sure you did.

"Would you like to be the one to lose your life because you kept me from the High Lord's side in his time of need?" I held up a hand as though I was going to unleash magic on him.

"No. Of course you may enter. It was my mistake." The man groveled and opened the door for me.

I nodded once, then stepped into an unfathomably large room. The door closed silently behind me.

There were beams of light shining down through the windows high overhead in the stone spires.

In the center of the room, in four expanding circles, stood a large group of men and women, all wearing cloaks that matched my own.

There were probably several hundred cloaked people in this room. I hoped that meant they wouldn't all recognize each other and immediately spot me as a fraud. I walked forward and made my way through the crowd towards the innermost circle.

In the center of this cavernous room, surrounded by hundreds of magic-wielding body guards, was my sister.

Lyric sat cross-legged and bound at the ankles in the center of an ornate ritual circle, which was inlaid on the stone floor.

Her skin was adorned from head to toe with elaborate markings that mirrored the runes in the circle. She wore a mostly sheer white dress that emphasized her form. Her golden hair had been intricately woven in braids and piled atop her head. She held her posture like a queen. Her expression was stoic despite the tears that filled her ethereal eyes.

Red fire raged inside of me as I barely contained the urge to unleash it on this room full of evil.

Keep it together Astrid. You need a plan.

I stood shoulder to shoulder with strangers and tried to mimic their expressions of reverence as they watched. Their focus was on a man with dark hair and a well trimmed beard. He looked like an Armani model in a luxury tailored three-piece suit—Alifar, I assumed.

He walked backwards around the perimeter of the ritual circle, dark magic emitting from his hands as he drew small patterns. Blood dripped from one of his hands and mixed with the magic that he was using. His profoundly handsome features focused on his task.

How do I get Lyric out of here without these people stopping us?

My mind was racing.

How do we escape without hurting her?

"Now," Alifar finished his spell and spread his arms wide, addressing his inner circle. "Anyone who crosses this circle dies."

Well, crap.

Alifar smiled and turned in my direction. My heart hammered in my ears. His expression was warm and his smile charming—right down to the dimple on one cheek.

"I appreciate you all coming on such short notice," He said, his eyes passing over me as he addressed the crowd. "I know some of you were taking time off with your families, and we'll get this done as soon as possible, so you can get back to that."

He gestured to a woman standing a quarter of the circle away from me. "Did your daughter have her baby yet?"

The woman bowed her head to the High Lord and murmured something I couldn't hear. Alifar tipped his head back in a genuine, friendly laugh. "Well, congratulations!"

This man was not at all what I had expected. I could imagine him, in his cream-colored suit, chatting with business partners at a charity dinner.

He didn't fit into the picture I'd drawn in my head of a man who inspired decades of rebellion and hate.

Alifar clapped his hands together. "Well! Let's get on with it, shall we?" He turned in a circle. "It's always exciting when we get to do these. I find I just can't wait any longer than I have to."

He stepped into the circle and approached Lyric, offering her a hand. "This one has been a long time coming."

Lyric took his hand and stood up. I could tell she was weak today. Everything in me wanted to rush to her side and steady her. The High Lord gently placed her hand in the crook of his elbow—the gesture of a gentleman escorting a lady. Lyrics expression was resolute, but I knew her well enough to see that she was afraid.

"Are you alright, my dear?" he asked her.

I gritted my teeth, watching him treat her like he cared about her when he was about to murder her.

"I want to be sure you're comfortable." He bent his head to look into her silver eyes. "Are you able to stand for a few minutes, now?"

"I'd like these shackles off my ankles," she said. Her voice was bold, and I felt a little in awe of her spirit.

He smiled at her, indulgent. "I really wish I could. It's the one thing I have to be a stickler about. I've found that as long as you stay exactly in the center of this circle, the entire thing will be completely painless for you."

Alifar patted her hand. "The ritual is very standard procedure. It's the same thing you would have done had you been becoming The Goddess of your realm, okay?"

If he weren't about to ritual sacrifice the only person in the world who mattered, I could see why people gravitated to him.

He spoke like a doctor, comforting a patient who was about to go under. "I have to interrupt the ritual at exactly the right time, so we by-pass the goddess step and the power diverts to me." Alifar brushed a tear from Lyric's cheek with his thumb.

Don't touch her.

My anger flared. The fire magic in my core threatening to unleash.

"You'll fade away into sleep without a care in the world."

His hand moved from her face to her shoulder. "But don't worry about all that. I've got it covered. All you have to do is stand here." He made sure she was steady before he left her side.

A plan was taking shape in my head. It was better to risk burning Lyric and heal her later, than to not use my greatest weapon.

Addressing the inner circle with a more sober expression, Alifar said, "I'll remind you that once the ritual begins, I have to release all of my own power for a brief time. In my weakened state, you are to guard me with your lives."

That was when I would attack. I prayed I would know the exact right moment.

His eyes scanned the crowd. "According to my informants, there's an assault on my front gate," Alifar sighed. "How it pains me to rush this experience, but we'll have to, so that you all can be available to help make an example of the criminals."

The High Lord's tone became more intense when he added, "Anyone who enters this room during the ascension ritual dies. Are we clear?"

I mimicked the people around me in bowing and responding—hating every moment of the pandering.

"I know you all understand the consequences of failure, so we won't bother with tainting this moment with that unpleasant business." Alifar smiled, then looked up at the windows high above. "My sources say the third moon has just crested the horizon. Take your positions!"

The guards around me all moved into a new formation, filling more of the room. Many of them turned to face the doors.

I took a step sideways and turned slightly, keeping the High Lord in my peripheral. I wasn't about to get any further from my sister.

Alifar addressed Lyric with a broad smile. "Shall we begin?"

. . .

I knew my best chance was to wait until he let his defenses down. Even then, I didn't know how my plan would succeed. I just knew I couldn't fail, or Lyric would die.

How will I know when it's time?

Will I be able to tell when his defenses are down?

My red magic flared. My heart was racing as the High Lord began to chant. Light of every color swirled around him and cocooned my little sister in magic.

I looked around, frantic.

Is it now?

Do I wait longer?

If I wait too long, it will be too late.

Time passed. Heartbeat after heartbeat.

Alifar knelt on the floor at my sister's feet, and his shoulders sagged slightly.

That might have been it.

Was that it?

I couldn't wait any longer. I stepped into the ritual circle just as Alifar was reaching up to Lyric.

"Don't touch her." I pushed back the cowl of my cloak.

Alifar and Lyric snapped their eyes to me.

"Astrid!" Lyric started sobbing. It was heartbreaking. I wanted to wrap her in my arms.

Be strong. Stay focused.

The High Lord's face filled with confusion, his eyes weak and exhausted.

Guards swarmed the circle. Not one crossed the line. But they sent magic flying from all directions. I flinched, but the attacks ricocheted off of the invisible barrier.

"How did you cross my barrier?" Alifar's voice was a mere shade of what it had been moments before.

My heart thrilled. *I got the timing right.*

"This will cost you your life." He panted and sagged back on his haunches.

As long as Lyric is safe.

I angled myself so that I would spare Lyric if possible.

Fire from my core finally burst free, encasing the High Lord. He chuckled weakly. The fire had no effect.

Crap.

New plan.

I drew on some of the training I'd gotten from Kai and kicked the High Lord in the head as hard as I could. He fell back. His face a mask of shock.

He got up, but stumbled.

I tried to kick him in the head. He caught my right foot, and twisted. My ankle snapped, shooting pain up my leg. I cried out as we both went down. My elbows hit the ground, hard. I slammed my good heel into his eye socket and then his neck twice. He went limp.

"Astrid!" Lyric screamed.

I whirled to see that her dress was burning and her leg along with it. She was trying to put it out without success.

I hobbled over, my broken ankle useless, and smothered the flames with my bare hands. The magic couldn't harm me.

"How do I stop the ritual?" I frantically searched around for something to break her free so we could leave the circle.

"No!" Lyric grabbed my hands. "Don't stop it."

"What?"

"I want to ascend." Her expression was serious.

My chest constricted. "No! Lyric, you don't understand—"

"I do." She nodded. "I know what it means."

"Someone else can do it."

Not my baby sister. Not the only person I have left.

"I want to be the one to do it." Lyric smiled at me, her eyes wet with tears.

"No." I shook my head, my chin quivering. "I can't lose you."

"You have to let me go."

I shook my head in denial. This couldn't be happening. Not after all I'd sacrificed, all we'd been through.

"Astrid, you've taken care of me all my life, and I'm so grateful." Lyric squeezed my hands. "Now I'm ready to be who I was born to be."

A desperate sob escaped my lips, as I looked at my little sister, who had long since outgrown me in height, as well as in courage.

This was not the plan.

Tears wet my cheeks.

Freya's words echoed in my mind. *'The only way to protect an Andeo is to have them ascend.'*

Letting her go will be like losing Mom all over again.

"*I can't.*"

Being alone... it was unspeakable. The one thing I could never bear.

"Astrid, it's time. ...Please?"

I recognized that firm look in her silver eyes. What she meant was, she was doing this either way. But she wanted my okay.

It's the only way to protect her.

Can I give her what she wants?

Can I stop her from making this choice?

Do I trust her to make this decision?

I thought of all the times she'd asked for more freedom, and I hadn't given it to her.

Her face was so steady, so sure. She was more ready than I had known. I was the fragile one. I was the one who wasn't ready.

The only thing in my power is to give her what she's asking for... or not.

I made my choice. There was no other way—I didn't want to regret our final moments together.

I wouldn't hold her back.

My chest tightened in protest.

The words seemed stuck in my throat.

It's the only way to protect her.

"Okay," I nodded. "I trust your decision."

As hard as it was to say, I knew I meant it.

"Thank you," she whispered.

I squeezed her hands. "I love you."

She sobbed once. "Ditto a million."

Our eyes remained locked, and Lyric smiled as she faded away in a blinding glow of light.

A concussive wave shook the earth.

Time froze. Or at least it seemed to.

She was gone.

Just like that.

. . .

Anguish filled my insides, cracking me open. I was flooded with a sorrow that couldn't be contained.

I realized the screaming in my ears was coming from me.

Power, turbulent as a wild sea, roiled through me. Light of every color erupted from my hands. Color and chaos permeated the entire inner sanctum, pouring out of me in an unending torrent. A whirlwind of ice and fire swept the room. Inner circle guards all around were destroyed or taking cover. The room shook with unbridled magic, the landscape of the floor shifting.

Rocks crashed down all around me. The remaining guards scrambling.

The light storm faded as the scream died from my lips. The room continued to crumble—devastation set in motion.

Several yards away, Alifar woke with a gasp when a rock crushed his leg. He threw his hands up and stared at me from behind an indigo force field—something like hate burning in his eyes.

My good leg trembled. I sagged to my knees, overcome with my grief.

A dark form dropped from above and landed beside me. In my haze I recognized Kai's familiar growl. His shadowy figure snapped the neck of a guard that was lunging to attack me with a blade.

Confusion and disbelief clouded my mind even as the Dragonborn's arms encircled me and he launched us into the air. I watched a sheet of slate shatter on the ground where I had been kneeling.

The roof of the inner sanctum was riddled with cracks.

Kai maneuvered through the debris still falling around us, hissing in pain when a sharp rock clipped one of his wings. Finally, we escaped through a break in the ceiling.

Once we were outside, he set me on a parapet of the castle that was still intact. I whimpered as my ankle protested my weight. Kai steadied me, then ripped the cloak in two, tearing it from my body and tossing it away. The black fabric shimmered as it fluttered down the castle wall.

When I tore my gaze away from the ruined cloak and saw Kai's skin, the sight snapped me out of my shock. His arms, hands, and neck were blistered where the cloak had touched him.

"You're burned!" I gasped.

"It's fine." He picked me up again.

"You shouldn't have touched that cloak."

"I knew what I was getting into before I did it."

His wings unfurled and propelled us into the moonlit sky.

Far below, I could see rebels and soldiers locked in battle.

Two brown dragons were fighting alongside the rebels. I recognized the smaller of the two—Sakashi. She carried Tyler on her back.

The young dragon sent a gust of fire into a mass of soldiers just before launching herself into the air behind Kai.

A dragonborn soldier dove after us. With her two clawed feet, the wyvern tore the soldier in half.

I looked away, nauseous from the gore.

Kai chuckled. "After what you just did to the inner circle, I'm surprised that bothers you."

Shame tightened my core. "You don't get to judge me."

He kept his eyes on the horizon. "I'll judge you as much as I want."

I narrowed my eyes at his profile. "Why did you come back?"

He shrugged, almost imperceptibly. "A sudden lapse in judgment."

"You shouldn't have ditched us."

If he had been there, maybe we could have gotten to Lyric earlier. Maybe it would have changed things.

I saw the burns on his skin and my irritation faltered.

I sighed. "At least you came back."

The dragonborn shrugged. "You raided a room of highly trained magicians and had the High Lord on the floor. I'm not sure you needed me."

"It didn't do any good... Lyric's gone."

"I know."

Sakashi pulled up along side us. Tyler wore an expression of dread. "Where's Lyric?"

I shook my head. "She's gone." My chin quivered. I saw the grief in Tyler's face before be looked away. A moment later, Sakashi beat her wings hard and pulled ahead.

Though he was far away, Tyler's anguished scream carried on the wind. The sound brought a wave of fresh tears to my eyes. I cried for Lyric. I cried for Tyler. I cried for my mom. And I cried for myself.

. . .

We flew for a long time, a dragon on either side of us; the larger dragon had caught up with us somewhere over the mountain range.

Eventually, Kai dropped down onto the larger dragon's back. He sat behind me, warm and solid. I sagged against his chest, allowing him to support my weight.

The only sound was a steady beating of dragon's wings as the wyvern carried us across the night sky.

SEVENTEEN

I had no memory of arriving at Khandra's house or collapsing into bed. When I woke, light streamed in through the window of Kai's room and a tiny face was standing next to the bed, staring at me. I blinked a few times. "Gemma! Hi."

She smiled and threw her arms around me. Surprise rippled through me. Belatedly, I put an arm around her small frame, in return.

The girl stepped back, and the warmth in her face communicated excitement.

She waved her hand at me to look and pointed at my leg. I moved the blanket aside and saw that my broken ankle was wrapped and set.

"Did Khandra use her healing magic on me?" I asked.

Gemma beamed and nodded.

"Did you watch her?"

Another nod. She bit her bottom lip—a gesture Lyric had often used when she was feeling shy. The thought was bitter sweet.

I gave her small hand a squeeze. "It's pretty cool, huh?"

I swung my legs to the floor and tested my ankle. I wasn't sure if I was supposed to walk on it yet, but it felt pretty good. Only a twinge of pain.

I followed Gemma into the main room of the cottage, where a large breakfast sat waiting on the large wooden table.

"Oh good. You're finally awake." Khandra's voice was stern, but I sensed an affection in her manner as she bustled around.

She added a large plate of sausages to the feast on the table. When she announced that Gemma helped bake the bread, the little girl's face beamed with pride.

I hadn't forgotten the promise I had made to Gemma's mother to get her home. Would Khandra be sad?

There was a man I didn't recognize in the corner, conversing with Kai. He was a little shorter than the dragonborn and not as broad or muscular. His pale face wasn't particularly handsome, but when he noticed me looking at him, a smile warmed his brown eyes and gave him a kind look.

"Hi there!" He sent a glance in Kai's direction, who raised his eyebrows a little before turning to face me as well. "Astrid, this is Ryder. Ryder, Astrid."

Ryder crossed the room in three long strides and held his hand out.

"It's good to meet you."

I reached out to shake his hand. He clasped it and brought his lips down to brush the back of my knuckles.

"I hope you slept well."

"I did, thanks." I glanced at Kai, who was watching—a scowl on his face. Clearly in a bad mood.

"If the rebels haven't killed the High Lord," Kai said, "he will rain hell down on the entire realm after what happened yesterday."

The change of subject was abrupt. But Ryder didn't seem phased.

"Yes," Ryder winked at me. "As much as I would like to get to know you better, you foreigners need to leave the realm and stay away until we know it's safe." He gestured to Tyler and I. "I've got a friend who is smuggling some people and gear to the Realm of Stars today. I can get you a spot on his ship."

I nodded in thanks. My heart soared at the thought of going home. I still held hope for my dream of the art institute.

"Actually..." Tyler said, interrupting my thoughts. "I think I'm going to stay here."

"What?" My face fell. "No!"

Loneliness washed over me. I'd already lost my sister. After everything we'd been through, I couldn't imagine Tyler not being there every day.

Tyler looked down at his hands. "I can't stand the thought of going back to a mundane life when Lyric is..." He trailed off.

Hearing Lyric's name made my heart constrict.

"Besides," Tyler shrugged. "Sakashi is here."

What about me? I forced the thought down. I wouldn't be selfish.

"What about your mom?" I said.

"She'll be fine." As though he'd read my thoughts, he added, "You could stay here too."

I shook my head. I wanted nothing to do with this realm.

It had taken Lyric from me. "I have a promise to keep to Gemma's mom."

At least I could do that much.

Tyler nodded, a bit sadly.

"Besides," I squared my shoulders. "I'm still hoping for a spot at the art institute."

He gently slugged my shoulder. "They'd be crazy not to let talent like yours in."

We all ate at the large wood table. I mostly pushed the food around on my plate, not really hungry. Kai seemed like he was in a bad mood, even the way he was eating was extra aggressive.

Tyler shared his story from the battle at Alifar's castle. Describing how he and I had gotten separated, and then he'd used his mind-link to Sakashi to summon the dragon.

"Before the dragons showed up," Tyler said, "I thought we were done for."

"Who was the second dragon?" Khandra asked.

"Sakashi brought her mother," Tyler said.

"Dragons rarely get involved with the conflict of another race," Ryder said. "That dragon must have really owed you."

"I like to think we have a strong bond," Tyler said. "With the help of the dragons, the rebels finally broke through the line and poured into the castle."

"Shame the dragons didn't hang around to help make sure the high Lord was dead," Ryder said.

Kai let out a soft growl of irritation.

"Well..." Tyler spoke quietly, "I told Sakashi the priority was getting Astrid and Lyric out."

At the mention of my sister, I finally asked Khandra and the others the only thing I was really interested in. "What happens to The Goddess after an andeo ascends?"

They all looked at each other. Silence settling over the group.

"Does anyone know?" I looked them each in the eyes.

They shook their heads.

"The only thing we know for sure," Khandra said, "is that a goddess is tied to her own realm."

I nodded once, processing the information. Lyric's spirit would be somewhere back in the Realm of Stars.

One more reason to get home as soon as possible.

After the meal, I told Kai that I was going to heal his burns. He didn't seem to appreciate my being forceful.

"The hell you are," was his response.

He and his grumpy ass headed out the back door.

I rolled my eyes and headed to the washroom. I got myself cleaned up and ready to head home.

Aside from the small satchel of things Khandra was sending with Gemma, there wasn't anything to pack. Tyler handed me my mother's cuff.

I brushed my thumb over the amber stone that had been returned to its place in the bracelet. Then hugged the boy who felt like a brother to me. My only remaining family.

"I want to know how you're doing once you get settled, okay?" I bumped his arm with my shoulder.

"I'm going to find a way to get this realm plugged into the internet, so I can get back to hacking." He grinned.

I chuckled and shook my head. "Of course you are."

"Once I've got it worked out, we'll be able to communicate."

"I'd like that." I gave his arm a squeeze.

I took my mother's beloved cuff and headed out back to look for Kai. When I rounded the barn, I found him chopping firewood.

He had his back to me, so I decided I could appreciate the man's physique for a few more swings of the ax before I was in danger of getting caught. The dragonborn was shirtless, and his skin glistened with perspiration, his hard muscles in pleasing motion, as he raised the ax above his head and brought it down. Desire flared in me.

Kai turned around and caught me staring, blatantly. I looked away, my face flushing.

Clearing my throat, I stepped forward. "I wanted to make sure you got this." I held out my cuff. "A deal's a deal."

He nodded and took it. "Can I ask you a question?"

His hard tone had me suddenly wary. "Okay…"

He jerked his chin towards me slightly. "You have every color of magic."

I shrugged. *Just more magic that I won't be able to control.*

"That wasn't a question." I raised my eyebrows at him, in challenge.

He folded his arms across his broad chest. "How?"

"I don't know." I shrugged.

"There's only one person in the history of all the realms who has every color, and it corrupted him." There was an edge of hostility in his tone. "How do you have all the colors?"

"I told you. I don't know."

He nodded once, then shoved the cuff in his pocket, and turned back to his task.

I looked at his injuries. The burns and scars that criss-crossed his skin did nothing to diminish his appeal, but my stomach twisted, knowing that the burns had been my fault. I didn't want to leave feeling like I owed him.

"Let me heal your burns." I reached out my hands to start.

"No."

Irritation flared in my core. "I'm just trying to help you."

"I don't want your help." His tone was full of anger.

I threw my arms up. "What is your deal?"

"I want you to leave." He turned to look at me.

I recoiled from the bitterness in his eyes. Apparently I had been really good at misreading this guy. I never knew what to expect, and I was over it.

He dropped his ax and headed back to the house, leaving me alone with the sting of rejection.

I hate him.

I hate this place.

I stood by the woodpile, fuming. One minute he was risking his life to rescue me, the next he was back to being an asshole.

He didn't risk his life for you, Astrid. He risked his life for the payment.

Well, he had what he wanted. I wouldn't spend time feeling sorry for him or his injuries.

When I got back to the cottage, Kai was in his room, so I didn't have to see him.

Good. I was already hurting enough.

"It's time to go," Ryder said, as he strapped his weapons belt on.

Khandra handed me Gemma's pack. "If you can't find her family, you bring her back to me." Her tone was sharp. "She has family here now, too."

I nodded.

She bent down to look into Gemma's eyes. "You are fierce. Remember, no matter how long it is until I see you again, I'll be thinking about you."

Gemma hugged the older woman. My throat tightened.

I took the little girl's hand, and we left, Tyler and Ryder leading the way. As we walked through the clearing, I couldn't keep myself from glancing back at the cottage. My breath caught when I saw Kai watching from his window, his hands braced on either side of the frame. Our eyes met, and the ache in my chest tightened. Hate no longer burned in his gaze. It had been replaced with something that frightened me far more. I recognized the agony in his eyes; it was a mirror of my soul...

Gemma's forward movement pulled on our clasped hands, and I snapped my gaze away from the dragonborn. I didn't dare look back again.

The town by the dock almost seemed deserted but for a few people who were skulking in the shadows.

"What happened here?" Tyler asked.

"News of Alifar's castle being breached has reached the outskirts of the realm," Ryder said. "People are scared."

We hurried to his friend's merchant ship. The captain was frantic to leave. "I have to get my family out of here." He hurried two young boys up the gangplank as he helped a sickly woman hobble along—his wife I presumed.

I turned to say a final goodbye to Tyler.

He handed me a folded paper. "For my mom."

I took it and slipped it into the pocket of my fireproof jacket.

I wrapped my arms around his neck. "Be safe, okay?"

He sniffed and cleared his throat. "Hey, take care of my bike for me."

"I will." I released my hold on my would-be, brother and boarded the ship.

The journey home was fascinating from the deck of the ship. We sailed on the open sea for two days. The waters were calm, and the sky was clear. Then with a shimmer of the light, the sky changed, and we were back on earth. Even if the captain hadn't warned me it was coming, I couldn't have missed it. We crossed the portal into the middle of a gray storm on the open sea. The storm struck fear into my whole body, but since Gemma was terrified, I put on a brave face for her. We went below deck to wait out the storm. We huddled together behind a couple of barrels where we had a makeshift bed in the supply room. I tried to distract her by teaching her how to play the Miss Susie hand-clap game. Lyric had loved that one. The game worked for a while. Eventually, I snuggled her and sang her songs until she fell asleep.

Hours later the captain came to tell us that the storm was past. His announcement was unnecessary—the lack of turbulence had calmed my nerves. According to the merchant, we had entered the Realm of Stars through the Bermuda Triangle into the North Atlantic. Apparently, it was a well-known portal between realms, but rarely used anymore. It was the one portal connecting all three of the realms, and it was risky.

"A slight miscalculation could send a ship to the Realm of Shadows, to never be seen or heard from again."

A tingle of fear rippled through me. "How can you be sure we aren't in the Realm of Shadows?"

The gruff man glared at me in answer to my question and turned to leave.

Evidently, he doesn't like his judgment to be questioned.

"How long until we reach land?" I asked.

"We'll make port in your Texas in two days." He closed the door behind him.

Crap. Texas is not exactly Kansas City, Missouri.

My mind set to work problem solving. Bus fare was probably cheaper than air. I ran through a myriad of ideas before my mind landed on one that seemed promising.

I smiled at Gemma who had just woken up. "We're almost home!"

Her eyes went wide, and she sprang up from her bed and grabbed my hands, jumping in excitement. Her joy was infectious. I jumped with her a couple of times. I laughed. Gemma laughed too. Hearing sound come from her was both unexpected and moving. I wrapped her in a hug and spun her around.

When I set her down, she rushed over to her small satchel

and rummaged around until she found what she was looking for. She walked back over and proudly presented me with a small object wrapped in cloth.

"What's this?" I asked.

She raised her eyebrows and pushed the small parcel into my hands.

"For me?" I said.

She nodded.

I began to unwrap the fabric. "Thank you—" I froze when the cloth fell away to reveal my mother's cuff, amber stone and all.

Confusion knit my brow, and I looked at the girl. "Did Kai give this to you?"

She shook her head and pointed at me.

"Did he tell you to give it to me?"

She nodded and smiled.

He risked his life for this, why would he give it back?

"Did he say anything else?" I asked.

She bit her lip and looked down.

"It's okay," I said, giving her a quick hug. "Thank you."

I tucked the cuff into my jacket pocket, rubbing my thumb over the stone. Warmth filled me.

EIGHTEEN

There is a part of every story that's never told. When the adventure is over and the characters have to find their way through healing after all the sacrifices and loss.

I had bartered with the merchant to get bus fare to KC for Gemma and I, in exchange for using my healing magic to help his wife. The captain had been more than happy with the bargain. The woman had some kind of septic infection. Healing her had been time-consuming and drained me of my energy. I'd slept most of the bus ride home with Gemma snuggled up next to me.

I hadn't cried since the Realm of Light, except for watching the reunion of Gemma and her father and brother. It had been touching, but also harrowing. We had all lost people we loved. When Gemma had finally broken her silence, it was to talk to her little brother. She had simply said his name, then melted into tears.

Gemma's father had sent a reward for her safe return. I had tried to refuse it but he wouldn't allow it. It was enough to live on for a couple of months, and I was grateful.

Stepping into the humid air of Kansas City had felt like coming home. I had lived so many places in my life, but it was here that felt like an anchor to my heart.

Weighed down with the grief of coming home without Lyric, I felt completely altered. It had been strange to find Tyler's bike untouched where I'd left it, as though the world had expected me to come back the same as I had left.

Now it seemed absurd to be afraid of the dangers of a motorcycle when life was so fleeting, no matter how careful you are. I'd come to understand you can't protect from every possible thing.

Upon my arrival home, there had been a last-minute acceptance letter from the Kansas City Art Institute in my mailbox. I'd gotten my full ride scholarship. It was everything I had ever wanted. I'd wished Lyric was here to celebrate with me. I wondered where she was, and what she was doing.

Lyric and I had both made choices in the Realm of Light that had changed our lives forever. I couldn't bring myself to regret letting her go—I never meant to hold her back. But in the two weeks that followed my being back in our empty apartment, I wondered if her choice had made her happy.

The plants that she kept on the counter had been neglected to near death. I summoned an orb of orange light for each one and watched the life come back to them as I gently pushed the magic into their leaves. I stepped back and smiled at the plants.

Lyric would have loved that.

After a week of grieving, I had gotten my paints out. At first I had painted because it felt like the only thing keeping me alive. After a while, I found that the painting was lifting my spirits and helping me process. I painted murals on my walls of things I had seen in the Realm of Light. Flowers, a sunset, trees, and mountains.

I found myself creating the likeness of the Dragonborn's piercing eyes. I spent hours on the details of his features, including the parts that he hid with his glamour.

When the piece was done, I stepped back with satisfaction. I'd captured his essence, even if the painting didn't do him justice. The likeness stared back at me, just as the man had the last time I'd seen him—the agony in his eyes.

"You are such a paradox," I said to the Kai on my living room wall.

"Who is that?" The voice came from behind me. I whirled around to find Lyric standing in my bedroom doorway. She looked strong and whole except that her body shimmered like she was an illusion. The light blue satin tank top she wore set off her silver eyes.

"Lyric?" I said, taking a step towards her. My heart in my throat.

"Seriously, Astrid, you captured broody and gorgeous."

She raised her eyebrows at the painting of Kai. Her smile was brilliant.

"You disappeared." I reached out to touch her. "How are you here?" My hand passed through her arm.

"I'm Mother Earth now." She gave a little curtsy, and I smiled. "I'm everywhere in this realm."

I bounced a little on the balls of my feet. "I didn't know you could visit!"

"Of course I was going to find a way to visit my favorite sister!"

We tried to clasp hands, and both laughed when the gesture was impossible.

"Dyami says I can appear in a corporeal form, but it's hard." Lyric scrunched up her face. "I'm not good at it yet."

"Who's Dyami?"

"She's the Goddess from the Realm of Light," she said. "She's helping me figure everything out."

I nodded. "Can you see Mom? Or talk to her?"

She folded her arms. "I'm not dead, Astrid. I'm a goddess."

I shrugged. "I was just hoping you could ask her why she kept all these secrets from us."

Lyric shook her head. "Sorry. I'm as clueless as you are. Unless we're talking about nature!" She got very animated as she described her ability to know what the earth needed and how to help it, anywhere on the planet.

"You seem really happy." I couldn't help but smile.

"I am!" She beamed. I could see that she meant it.

Her body flickered like it was glitching. "I've got to go."

"But you just got here." My face fell.

"I'll get better at this and hopefully I can stay longer next time." She shrugged.

I nodded and smiled. "Okay, I'll see you soon?"

"Of course!" She winked.

I smiled. "I love you!"

"Ditto a million!" She laughed and then she was gone.

My grin was so big it hurt my cheeks. Peace washed away the pain I had been living in.

Later that day, I spread a blanket on the living room floor. I sat cross-legged in the middle, facing the mural I'd painted. Afternoon sun bathed my face in warmth as I took in all the colors that I'd painted to mimic the Realm of Light.

I let my eyes flutter closed, and I searched inward. Deep down, I found my red magic. The now-familiar power roiled in me—still harsh and untamed—but now I didn't fear it. My new perspective on my red magic was that it had saved my life more than once. I silently inclined my head, sending the magic respect and gratitude. The red light shimmered through my senses in response—a dance of light. It turned from red chaos to an intricate scarlet aura.

Whoa.

This was a shift I had never felt before. I opened my eyes and looked at my arms and legs. My red aura was visible and gently moving around me, it felt like balance.

"Okay," I whispered. I sat frozen. The thrill of a breakthrough coursing through my body. "I think I get it." A small laugh escaped me, and I let loose the smile on my face.

Closing my eyes once more, I searched for more colors. I

easily found the comfortable orange magic. Traveling up through my core, it took great concentration, but, eventually, I found yellow, then blue, and indigo, and finally, violet in my head.

I couldn't remember what Khandra said each color could do, but I was itching to find out.

I struggled to find the green that was supposedly near my heart, based on how the chakras were laid out. Eventually I thought I might have glimpsed it, but it was so faint, I couldn't be sure it wasn't my imagination.

The strain of tapping into my magic had me feeling bone tired. When I opened my eyes, I realized I might not even have the strength to get off the floor.

Maybe my next apartment needs to have a stone floor for this.

I ended up just laying down on the blanket, where I stayed the entire night.

The next morning it was the first day of classes. I'd been late to register, so I had taken what I could get, and I didn't even have all of my supplies yet. I didn't care; I was just excited to finally go. I put what supplies I already had into Lyric's old backpack and skipped down to the parking lot.

It was a beautiful day. Contentment spread through my chest as I climbed onto Tyler's motorcycle. I noticed my van, sitting forlorn, a few spaces away. It reminded me of the last day at my old job and of the cowboy soldier I'd met. At the time, I had resigned myself to the fact that I could never open myself up to someone like him.

Letting Lyric go had felt like something I'd never survive. But she wasn't lost, and I had survived. We were both okay. I thought of Jen, and Tyler, and Kai, and Gemma, and all of the times I had kept myself at a distance from people.

I told myself it was to protect Lyric.

Who am I protecting now?

I shook my head, not wanting to face the ugly truth that was right in front of me.

My heart started beating faster as my nerves protested where my mind was going.

Maybe we'll never lose everyone we love because there are always people to love, if we let them in.

I'd lived so long holding too tight to my mom and Lyric, afraid to lose them. Afraid to get attached to anyone else.

I drew in a breath and held it for a beat. My thoughts gaining momentum.

I bent down to rummage through the trash in my door for a barbecue-stained business card.

When I found what I was looking for, I saved Captain Jeff Miller's number as a contact in my phone. Hands shaking, I sent him a text before I could talk myself out of it.

Drinks sometime?"

What am I thinking?
This is a bad idea.

Who is this?

This is my chance to back out.

Get it together Astrid. Normal people do stuff like this all the time.

> Astrid Stone.

> Server at Downtown BBQ...

> I passed out...

Maybe he won't remember and we can just forget the whole thing.

> Yes!

> I absolutely remember you! Prettiest girl I've ever seen.

My stomach flipped. A smile warming my cheeks.
Oh my gosh, I don't know how to respond.
I watched the bubble on my phone that told me he was typing something else. I wished Lyric was here to help me; I had no idea what I was doing.

> I was really hoping I'd hear from you.

> I'm out of town for a couple of days...
> Does Friday work for you?

I checked my empty calendar.

> Sure.

That was it?
I did it?

I did it!

My first date.

Lyric is going to be shocked. I can't wait to see the look on her face when I tell her.

I bit my bottom lip and smiled.

thanks for reading!

To find book 2, go to

www. ajblanch. com

Thank you to

Kyle—the love of my life.
Catherine Herrick, Joseph Blanch, Charis Emrich, James Blanch, Becky Tolman, my siblings, my in-laws, and my friends. I have an amazing group of support! Janeen Ippolito, editor extraordinaire. (She didn't edit this page. Hope there aren't too many mistakes!)
My kids—good job feeding yourselves when I was working in the office.
My beta readers.
xoxo

About the Author

AJ Blanch discovered writing back when she found she could procrastinate her math homework by distracting her mother with an original poem or anecdote.

She now crafts stories of fantasy, magic, and romance. She still avoids doing math.

Some of AJ's favorite things are, family game night with her man and their four kids, horses, and delicious baked things.

Made in the USA
Monee, IL
31 August 2023

41929020R00173